SHIMMER

Crown of Fae Book One

SHARON ASHWOOD

Cover art by The Illustrated Author.

Edited by Cynthia Shepp

Map by Zenta Brice

Shimmer/ Sharon Ashwood—1st ed.

PRAISE FOR SHARON ASHWOOD

Sharon Ashwood is all that is good and right in the paranormal romance genre.

— BITTEN BY BOOKS

Fast paced and captivating... chemistry is immediate and undeniable, and the love scenes are scorching hot.

— PUBLISHERS WEEKLY

Multiply the Wow Factor, the Dark Forgotten saga must continue!

— SINGLE TITLES

This is a splendid way to spend your precious leisure time!

— ROMANTIC TIMES BOOK REVIEWS TOP PICK!

SHIMMER

Three wishes, two warriors, one chance at redemption

Fae martial artist Alana Beech demands justice when her teammate dies during a rigged fight—but no one cares. Injured and alone, Alana is forced to accept a last-chance job at a curiosity shop. There she finds a magic lamp—and a spark of hope—in a box of abandoned junk.

Ronan is a dragon prince imprisoned during the destruction of the fae homeland. He's the genie bound to the lamp and forced to grant three wishes to every comer. As handsome as he is hazardous, Ronan joins Alana's search for answers.

While their alliance turns passionate, Alana's quest reveals a mystery that goes far beyond murder. The lamp is a lethal weapon, and Ronan's enemies are hunting for him. Alana will do anything to guard her lover's back, but sometimes a warrior's courage—like the genie's wishes—carries an unexpected price.

N
IMRAGEN
GRAY MOUNTAINS
WESTERING RIVER
MARGIT BAY
POMANDINE
BLACK LAKE
HAWKSGATE RIVER
HEARTRUIN RIVER
ELDABAN
GREAT DESERT
SERPENT RIVER
RAVAGED LANDS
THE FAERY REALM

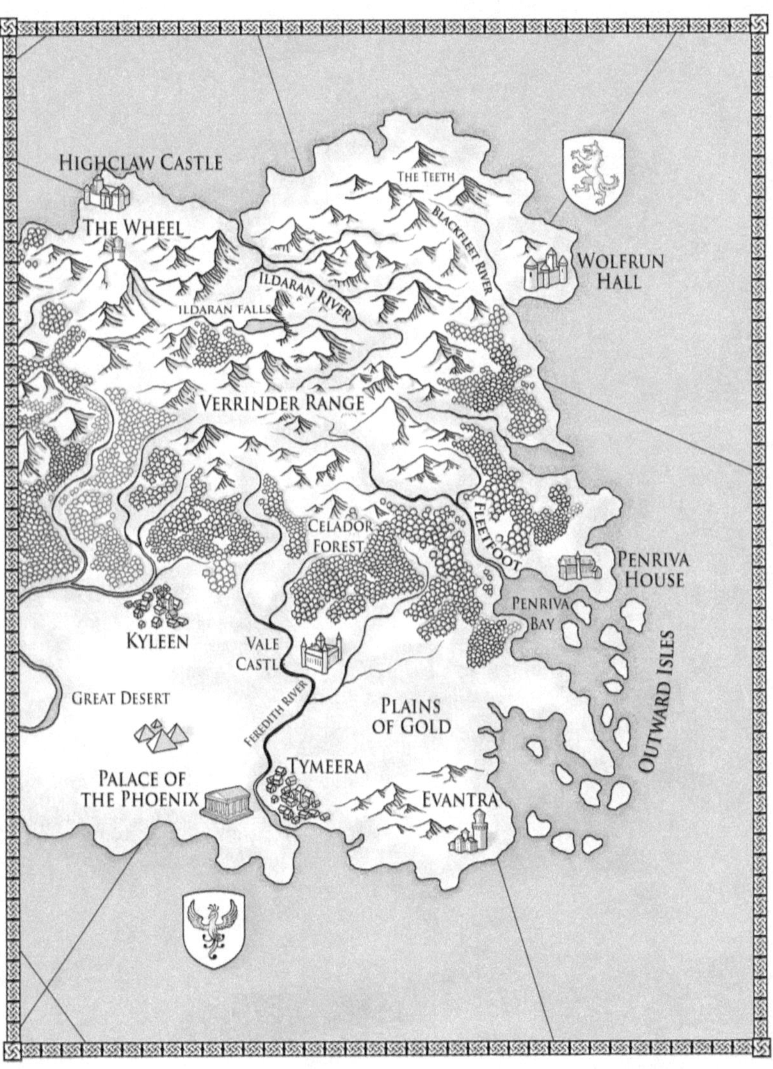

HIGHCLAW CASTLE
THE WHEEL
THE TEETH
WOLFRUN HALL
ILDARAN RIVER
ILDARAN FALLS
BLACKFLEET RIVER
VERRINDER RANGE
CELADOR FOREST
FLEETFOOT
PENRIVA HOUSE
PENRIVA BAY
KYLEEN
VALE CASTLE
OUTWARD ISLES
GREAT DESERT
FEREDITH RIVER
PLAINS OF GOLD
PALACE OF THE PHOENIX
TYMEERA
EVANTRA

PROLOGUE

C*enturies ago*
The Faery Realm

AIR SNAPPED UNDER THE DRAGON'S WINGS AS HE CAUGHT THE
updraft, sailing higher. Sun gleamed on his pearly white and gray
scales, turning them to rivers of iridescent blue and green. The fae
dragons of the Wheel were massive, fearsome creatures of breath-
taking beauty. They were also the lords of the land, and they
protected what was theirs with fire and fang.

The extra lift gave the dragon a better view, and he twisted his
sinuous neck to catch a glimpse of his quarry. *There.* Anger flared
through him, bitter and red as spilled blood. There was the
enemy, swarming like rats beyond the sharp-edged mountains.
Hiding like...

Shades. Eternal enemies of the fae.

With a snort of steam, the dragon angled into a circling dive,
wind roaring past his membranous wings. He was Ronan, Prince
of Bright Wing and commander of his kin. After King Vass, his

father, Ronan was the greatest of the dragons who patrolled the sky against the Shades.

He snarled, the urge to protect thundering wildly in his blood as land, sea, mountain, and desert stretched below him. This was *his* world. His family governed the air fae. They sat on the council that met on the flat-topped mountain called the Wheel. The High King of Faery ruled the realm, but only with the council's advice. The system was fair, if not perfect, and it had kept the peace for thousands of years.

Until now. Until war.

Ronan crossed the ridge of the first mountains and then flew low, hugging the tips of the tall firs. Recent battles had taught him caution. Shades were related to the fae, for they spoke the same tongue and bore similar shapes. And yet, their souls were forged of a different metal—one that was blackened and twisted. If the fae of the Wheel fought to protect their own, the Shades attacked for the pure pleasure of chaos.

The trees gave way to the green sweep of the valley. Ronan dipped with the land, keeping as inconspicuous as a huge white dragon could be. He'd seen the smoke from afar. Now as he saw the source, his anger congealed to ice. There had been a village on this hillside. All that remained were the blackened stumps of houses, the folk and their animals turned to ash where they stood. Some had been scrambling for the woods, others huddled for a last moment of comfort. Not even the dovecots remained.

Something inside Ronan cracked. Pain welled, ferocious in its intensity. These villagers had been innocents in need of his protection. Instead, they'd perished—not even by the cleansing fire of a dragon, but by something that left the stench of corruption behind.

Shades. They were gone now, moved on to destroy a different village in another valley. But how? How were they coming and going undetected?

Roaring his fury, Ronan beat his wings hard, climbing so

quickly he seemed to challenge the sun itself. When he rose to the highest place the air would hold him, he spied what another of the mountain valleys held. In one bowl-shaped hollow that lay amid the jagged rock, there should have been a lake of crystal water. Instead, a midnight blackness shimmered in its place.

He alighted on a high ridge, where he had the best view—but where he was also the most visible. With an instinctive flash of magic, he shifted. It took hours to take his dragon form, but almost no time at all to assume a human body. Now much less conspicuous, he crouched where the ragged rocks gave him cover. Like all the noble fae, Ronan was tall and well-made, his warrior's physique heavy with muscle. He ducked his dark head, peering down on the scene below.

It wasn't the cold mountain wind that turned his bare flesh to ice. An army of thousands—of tens of thousands—marched from the inky waters of the lake. Except they weren't waters at all, but a doorway made of reflection magic.

The Shimmer. He'd read about it in books, and he knew what it could do. This was Shade magic.

It spelled the end of his world.

$$\maltese \quad I \quad \maltese$$

P*resent Day*
The Human Realm.

ALANA BEECH PUSHED THE ELEVATOR BUTTON WITH ALL THE enthusiasm of a felon on her way to the gallows. When the doors shuddered open, she gave an audible sigh, hitched up her shoulder bag, and prepared for the ordeal ahead.

It had been years since she'd searched for a job, but, after a month recuperating, she needed a paycheck fast. Sadly, few companies wanted a washed-up fighter giddy on painkillers. She'd suffered two knife wounds, along with a whole lot of bites and scratches, in a no-holds-barred tag-team match with two cat shifters. Underground fights offered no compensation for injuries and the losers were, well, losers—in more ways than Alana could count. That fight had smashed her entire life to pulp.

But the past was off-limits today, because even invalids had to pay the rent. No, today was about survival and moving forward, and that meant finding work. When a fighter was too hurt to perform, it was time to think outside the box, and Alana had ideas. While she had nothing in common with the hungry young corporate sharks who haunted the business district—except maybe the hungry part—they needed people with her talents. All she had to do was convince them of the fact.

The elevator dinged, the doors groaned open, and she stepped into a beige-on-beige hallway. At the end of the corridor, she could see the sign for the Wildwood Employment Agency, where the overhead light flickered like a dying firefly. She forced her feet into a confident march, though her wounds still throbbed with each beat of her pulse. Hiding her weakness was essential if she wanted to get hired, but she was used to masking pain.

To the casual eye, Wildwood was an old-school agency for temporary office workers. To those in the know, it did the hiring for all the fae businesses in town. Alana's old coach, Henry, had called in a favor to get her the appointment. He'd been the only person in her corner once her universe swirled down the drain.

When she arrived, the door creaked open of its own accord. A wave of gooseflesh swept up her body, signaling the presence of magic. Warding spells, probably, checking to see if she had an invitation. Forcing a smile, she went inside. A reception counter faced the door, with a tweed couch and chairs framing a waiting area to her right.

"How may I help you?" asked a wizened figure seated at reception. As Alana approached, it raised a narrow, wrinkled face framed by ropes of frizzy white hair. Bones, beads, and the occasional paper clip decorated the trailing locks.

Goblin, Alana thought, cataloguing the threat out of habit. Despite their wispy frames, goblins were strong and could deliver a nasty bite. Like almost all fae, they were capable of hiding their appearance from human eyes. She could see what it was, but she was fae. "I have an appointment with Mr. Barleycorn."

Rather than consult the computer, the creature lifted a thick tome onto the counter and opened it to a page marked by a ribbon. Dates and times divided the pages in flowing indigo script. Maybe the tech was just for show? Or maybe the handwritten record was for special, off-the-books clients like her? It would make sense to keep separate listings, since humans weren't supposed to know about the magical world.

The goblin ran a clawed finger down the entries, stopped at a line, and consulted its shiny gold pocket watch. "Your appointment was at two o'clock. It is now two-oh-five."

"My apologies," she said quickly. "Traffic."

The creature peered over the wire rims of its glasses. The eyes were yellow and slitted like a goat's. "Punctuality is a predictor of professionalism."

Alana's cheeks heated. She was late because it hurt to move. Dressing was agony, and climbing the steps of the bus even worse —but she wasn't about to admit that. Weakness paved the road to extinction. "I'm sorry."

The goblin sniffed and slammed the book shut, then rose to its full, spindly height—which was still a head shorter than Alana's five-foot-seven. It wore a forest-green suit, complete with bow tie and yellow waistcoat.

"I brought a résumé, if Mr. Barleycorn would like to see it." She handed over the pages, and the goblin accepted them as if they smelled of rotten fish.

"Take a seat," it said, gesturing toward the couch. "I will see if Mr. Barleycorn is still available."

"Thank you."

The goblin sniffed before disappearing through the door behind its desk. Alana sat, feeling the scratchy tweed fabric of the couch right through her skirt. Her fingers crushed the leather strap of her bag in a death grip.

It was then she realized there was someone else waiting. He was well into middle age, with a lined face and slicked-back hair gone gray at the temples. He wasn't a full-blooded fae, but he had the characteristics of one of the mountain tribes—sturdy but not overly tall, with startling dark blue eyes and a faint indigo cast to his skin that only other fae would notice.

He moved closer, taking a seat on the couch to her left. "Hi. I'm Billy Randall." He thrust out a hand.

"Alana. Pleased to meet you." She shook, sizing him up. *Left-handed, favors the right leg when he moves, smiles too much—a salesman?*

"Are you here for the Martigen interviews?" He seemed faintly worried.

"No."

Her answer must have meant she wasn't competition because his brow relaxed. "What are you here for, then?"

"A gig in security."

"An analyst?" He fidgeted with his tie, patting it into place.

The guy had all the nervous tics of someone waiting for an interview. Although the last thing she wanted was small talk with a stranger, she took pity on him. "More likely I'll end up on the practical side," she said. "That's where my experience is."

Randall's jaw dropped slightly as he ran his gaze up and down, reassessing her slim figure. "No kidding?"

She allowed herself a smile. People always confused size with strength. "No kidding."

"You don't look like a bodyguard. You're too pretty."

"Thank you, I guess."

She'd tried to pull off an acceptable appearance. Long sleeves covered the stitched-up knife wound that tracked from her left wrist past the bend of her elbow. Her skirt and blouse were plain but appropriate, her fair hair brushed into a sleek braid that hung down her back, and her makeup just dark enough to emphasize her wide gray eyes. Today, she'd armed herself for a different kind of battle.

"To be honest," she added, "this will be a change of career."

He studied her then, eyes narrowing. "You said your name was Alana. Are you Alana Beech? The Incorruptible?"

Reluctantly, she nodded, acknowledging her stage name. If

Billy Randall recognized her, he was acquainted with the underground games.

"That last fight..." He trailed off, shaking his head.

There were a lot of ways to end that sentence. *Finished her career. Killed her partner. Broke her.*

Randall grabbed her thigh with iron fingers, leaning in so close she could feel his breath on her face. Yup, that grip said mountain fae. He could crush rocks with those fingers. She barely stopped a gasp of pain.

"That last fight cost me *everything*," he snarled. "Every last dollar and then some."

So he'd gambled and lost. Did that have anything to do with why he was here, hoping for a job? Alana felt a flash of sympathy, but the pain in her leg squashed it.

"Remove your hand," she said quietly.

"Who paid you off?" He was breathing hard, his eyes boring into hers with sheer desperation. Her stomach fluttered with dread. All the chaos from that night came flooding back, the creeping conviction that something was horribly wrong with the match. She'd known it before the first bell, like a bad smell in the air. Now Alana could taste the terror again, lingering like an oily poison. She'd watched Tina, her fighting partner, sink to her knees, her eyes going dark in death.

It should never have happened. *Betrayal.* Waves of raw emotion pounded in, letting Alana know her true healing hadn't even begun. The wounds of the body were just the tip of a hurt that went far deeper. Tears pooled in her eyes.

Blinking hard, she put her hand over Randall's to pry it away. "You don't seriously think I wanted to lose like that?"

"Who paid you?" His grip tightened another degree, setting her nerves on fire.

In one swift movement, Alana twisted, using the momentum to rise. A second later, she'd pinned him, one arm twisted at his back and his cheek squashed into the tweed couch cushion. "I told you to let go."

Randall replied in gutter fae that should have melted the paint from the walls.

Alana had heard it all before. "You're boring me."

"Who paid you to lose?" he demanded again.

"You think if I got a big payoff I'd be here, looking for work? Use your head."

Her point made, she let Randall go. He sprang away, spots of color high on his cheeks. She straightened her clothes, brushing away any wrinkles.

"Bitch," Randall grumbled, but he did it under his breath this time.

The goblin chose that moment to return. It gave an annoyed cough. "Ms. Beech?"

She turned away from Randall, blanking him from her thoughts. If she didn't, she'd do something that would get her thrown out, arrested, or both.

The goblin flicked its gaze between them with ill-disguised curiosity. "Mr. Barleycorn informs me that he is willing to honor the remaining fifteen minutes of your appointment."

"Then let's go." Without a backward glance, Alana followed the creature into the private part of the office suite. Despite the faint scent of magic in the air, nothing seemed remarkable. Landscapes on the walls. Oak doors with brass nameplates. The smell of somebody's reheated lunch. They stopped outside a corner office.

"Remember this is your one chance," the goblin said in dire tones. "Take whatever job he offers you and like it. Mr. Barleycorn never sees a candidate twice." Then it turned and retreated to its station in the front room.

"Great pep talk." Alana's temper stirred, along with a bad case of the butterflies. Sucking in a breath, she boldly went where thousands of desperate job-seekers had gone before.

Her steps went silent as her heels met the deep pile of the carpet. The office was huge, with a massive mahogany desk and bookcases that reached the ceiling. A woven map of the Faery homeland hung on the wall. Alana recognized the territories of the fae tribes from grade school: air, water, fire, and earth each in a primary color. Humans probably thought the map was from a fantasy book. They might as well—it was all ancient history now. The high king was dead, and the fae exiled to the human world. She gave the map no more than a moment's consideration, focusing on more immediate concerns.

Barleycorn himself was dark haired and impeccably dressed, down to his monogrammed cufflinks. He appeared to be an ordinary human, but Alana knew better. She'd seen him around the fae community all her life, an aloof and important man with his fingers in every fae business and a few human ones, too. But the executive image didn't fool her. Barleycorn was as fae as moonlight and dew circles, and was probably older than dirt.

As she approached, he closed the file folder before him and folded his hands. Maybe the gesture was meant to convey patience, but she felt like a child called to the principal's office.

She came to a halt on the other side of the massive desk. "Thank you for seeing me, Mr. Barleycorn."

"My pleasure." He tapped the file folder lightly. "You have quite the history, Ms. Beech."

"I also have skills."

That seemed to amuse him, though his smile was the thinnest crescent. She itched to fold her arms over her stomach, to protect her vulnerable places from his scrutiny. Instead, she forced her hands to hang loose at her sides, her back straight and chin up.

"Henry Blackwell called me," he said. "You're here because you're out of options."

Henry, her coach. He'd told her she'd never fight again, and her body had seconded the opinion. Part of her still refused to believe it. "I need a job, sir."

"And you don't know how to do anything but fight."

She set her jaw. "I can still work in security."

He frowned, picking up a paperweight from his desk. It was a marble dragon, each scale exquisitely carved. "Do you know what happened to the air fae, Alana?"

She blinked, wondering where he was going with this. "They came here, like everyone else."

"The little ones did. The pixies and flower fae, but the dragons stayed behind to fight the Shades. They shared more with the dinosaurs than long tails and bad breath. Oh, yes, they were strong, beautiful, and amazing creatures, but they were proud to the point of idiocy. Hence, you will never meet a dragon." He put the paperweight down. "Learn to adapt to circumstances, Alana, or face the consequences."

"I know I can't fight like I used to, but..."

"You're an orphan, a foundling of dubious pedigree, who never even attempted higher education. You want me to find you a job guarding important fae, yet your magic abilities are all but nil. Plus, your body is broken. You're attempting to hide the agony of simply standing here, but I can sense it like a shrieking siren. What can you possibly offer?"

Alana's body tensed, her heart beating faster. It was as if she'd suddenly found herself on splintering ice, and hesitation would get her drowned. But how was she supposed to respond?

He'd asked a good question. His words summoned old memories—schoolyard taunts, the disappointed eyes of her adopted parents. She'd been a useless mongrel with zero talent for the basic spells any fae toddler could do. Then she'd learned to fight better than anyone else, and doors to fame, if not exactly fortune, had opened.

Now those doors had slammed shut again. "I need a job to survive."

"Why should that matter to me?"

Light dawned. He was testing her, seeing how well she

conducted herself under pressure. Still, angry heat flared in her gut. "Maybe my welfare doesn't matter to you, but it does to me."

"Why?"

Another good question, but she knew the answer instantly. If she survived, then she could discover what really happened during that fight. She owed it to Tina to find out.

That wasn't his business. "My reasons are my own."

"And I have a reputation. I can't recommend you to a client unless I know who you are."

"You have my file."

"That's words on paper. I need to know you'll see your work through to the bitter end."

Alana raised a brow. "Sounds like fun."

Barleycorn nodded slowly. "Something is motivating you besides money. Something greater than the pain in every one of your joints."

Revenge. With a wrench, Alana realized she ached for it. She'd known it before, but in a fuzzy way. Now it was a crystalized goal with a name. She stared at Barleycorn, wondering what he wanted her to say. The guy had opened her up as if she were a shellfish. Was he spinning some kind of magic? Hypnosis? Mind-reading? She wasn't fae enough to tell. Just another of her deficiencies.

Abruptly, she ran out of patience. The famous Barleycorn was a first-class jerk. She braced her hands on his big, shiny desk and leaned forward, hoping she left fingerprints. "You want insight? I need a job. I can't afford to be picky. I'll take whatever you have to offer."

He sat back with a feline smile, as if she'd cut past the job-seeker posturing and finally given a worthwhile answer. "You truly don't care what that job is?"

"Within reason. I'll take anything that's honest."

That seemed to satisfy him. "Then sit down."

Alana glanced around in surprise. A red leather chair had materialized where there had been none before. She sank into the soft cushion, her aches and pains easing. The relief was more magic, but she welcomed it.

Barleycorn eased a file from the bottom of a stack teetering in his inbox. "This isn't much, but it should keep the wolf from the door."

❈ 2 ❈

C *enturies ago*
  The Faery Realm

RONAN ROARED HIS DEFIANCE, STABBING HIS SPEAR AT AN enemy's chariot. Horses shied, the driver veering away in a plume of dust and mocking laughter. Ronan spun, his short cape swirling, his weapon ready to slash. A dragon could do more damage to the enemy and, at any other time, he would have taken to the skies in his beast form. But his magic was exhausted from this fight—every spell drained in defense of the kingdom. He was just a warrior now, saving his last scraps of power for a final gamble. Ronan told himself the soldiers needed to see him at the front of the charge, sword in hand and shoulder to shoulder with his men.

They needed courage, because the tide of war had turned. At the start, the fae had been victorious, but now their losses were severe. Most were fleeing the land, but the dragons were making a stand. They chased the enemy across kingdoms to confront Harin

Blacktongue, war leader of the Shades. Now they'd engaged his army, but Ronan had yet to clap eyes on Harin himself. These days, the man was a ghost.

The sun glared upon the desert lands of Faery, flaring brightly where it caught the gleaming armor of the fighters. The chariot was turning, getting ready for another attack. Ronan's practiced eye could see the horses had been used hard, for foam flecked their midnight flanks. That didn't mean they wouldn't trample him to a paste. And if the beasts didn't kill him, there were the long, flashing blades that extended from the chariot wheels like twirling swords. Those could mow him down like a stalk of wheat.

It was down to basics. He had his spirit, his spear, and the twin swords sheathed at his back. His own chariot lay in pieces, the horses fled in panic. Grotesquely outnumbered, Ronan's army had cut the Shades in two. Yet, the enemy refused to surrender. Their magic was darker, their lust for violence unthinkable.

This was Ronan's final stand. He thought of his family—the mother and brothers and sisters who had given their lives in this war, his remaining little sister, and his despairing father. A small inner voice pointed out that a glorious death sounded far better in a ballad than it did in reality. Ronan cursed, clenching the spear tighter to hide the tremor in his hands.

The war chariot charged, blades spinning as the wheels turned. Even in the din of battle, he heard the pounding hooves and jangle of harness. The image of the driver shimmered, reforming into a tall figure in a golden helmet. Shock froze Ronan for a split second.

Harin! No one ever saw the war leader's face since he'd donned that helmet he wore. Some said he was cursed, others proclaimed him an empty hunger without form.

Satisfaction bloomed in Ronan's mind. *Nonsense.* He knew Harin could die, for Ronan had known him long before the Shades had corrupted him. Once upon a time, he'd been a water fae and an old friend. Once, he'd lived by the lake in the mountain where the armies of the Shades had first appeared.

The gold of Harin's armor shone against the cloudless sky, making him an excellent target. Hot, dusty air burned in Ronan's lungs as he bellowed his rage. Harin screamed back, swerving to cut him down. At the final moment, Ronan jumped, heaving his spear. He tucked and rolled in the air, the world blurring to a jumble of dust and iron-shod hooves. But somehow, he had timed it wrong. As he landed, the spinning blades on the chariot wheels whirred past, slicing a strip of skin from his thigh. Heat flared, followed by a wave of pain as he bounced to his feet, ready to keep fighting.

But he stumbled, hitting the packed earth hard. A grunt of agony leaked through his clenched teeth, as much from the blow to his hopes as his body. The chariot's wheel blade had cut through more than skin. It had flayed his muscle to the bone, crippling him in the process.

Ronan closed his eyes, refusing to let despair claim him. The agony in his leg meant nothing. Flesh was flesh. Defeat was dishonor. He would fight on just as soon as he could stand—which wasn't happening at the moment.

Harin Blacktongue leaped from the carriage. The war leader's presence sucked the desert heat from the air around them—proof enough he commanded the darkest magic. An unseen force hammered Ronan face-first into the dirt. Then Harin's boot heel ground between Ronan's shoulder blades, crushing the air from his lungs.

"Your army seems to be running away," Harin observed. His voice was dark velvet, surprisingly quiet for such a huge, muscular frame. "So much for their loyalty, dragon prince."

Ronan remained silent. Even if he could have drawn breath to reply, there was nothing to say.

Harin leaned down, shifting his weight to cause maximum discomfort. "From the generals down to the lowliest foot soldier of the fae, I crushed your little tribe. Those who did not die fled deep into the mountains and forests to weep and lick their wounds. Some even captured a Shade and then forced him to open the Shimmer to a distant land. But here you are, little princeling, desperate to save the day. Who do you think you are?"

"If you are going to kill me, have done with it." Ronan longed for his dragon form. Then he could roast Harin and take to the skies, but it was fruitless wish. Even if he had the strength to shift right then, a change so profound took more than a limerick and a pinch of pixie dust. It took hours, and his time had run out.

Harin laughed, the sound holding both sadness and cruelty. "Did you think I would grant you an honorable death, old friend?"

"You were one of us!"

"And since that time, my new lords have lifted me out of obscurity and into glory. I'm not sentimental in the least."

Harin drew back, allowing Ronan to push himself up. Agony stabbed from his wound, where large blood vessels had been slashed through. He should have bled to death by now, but the war leader was sparing his life through magic. Why? Slowly, painfully, he shifted his position to confront the enemy—or at least his golden armor. A latticework grill hid Harin's features. He might have been ordinary, repulsive, or invisible for all Ronan could detect.

Harin's army milled some distance away. A smaller entourage waited closer to hand, servants and personal guards bearing fierce-looking weapons. Two of the largest soldiers flanked the war leader. They were Shades—tall and almost slender despite their armor. Long hooded cloaks fell to their ankles, the hoods drawn up to hide their faces. They hovered close to the war leader, blades drawn and ready. Even though Ronan was wounded, Harin was being cautious.

He glared into Harin's golden mask. "You think you're lifted into glory? You're nothing but the boot boy to the King of Shades."

"Your arrogance amuses me," Harin said. "It always has."

"I'm protecting my own."

"So you are. No one else has presumed to attack me directly, but of course you had to try. For that presumption, I have a special use for you."

"Use?" Ronan had gone beyond fear into a kind of blankness, as if this were happening to someone else.

"You don't believe I would waste a creature with your power, do you?"

Harin gestured, and an aide in dark livery brought him a wide-mouthed goblet. Ronan expected Harin to drink—though the helmet would have been an issue—but instead, the war leader drew near. Harin signaled to the guards beside him and they grabbed Ronan's arms. He struggled, but they held him tight. Harin brought the goblet close. Ruby wine shimmered inside, reflecting Ronan's face.

His heart jumped in panic. Shades used mirror magic, and this was as good as any looking glass.

Harin bent so the golden mask stared into Ronan's face, and Ronan could see the flicker of glowing violet eyes. "If you had one wish right now, what would that be, dragon prince?"

Freedom. Futile though it was, he scrabbled for his magic, straining to summon his dragon form. With claw and fang and fire, he could be done with Shades.

"Too late," Harin said in his velvety voice. To his horror, Ronan understood that somehow Harin had gained the power to read his mind.

The reflection began to tear the white dragon from inside Ronan. It should have been impossible—it wasn't as if the two halves of his being were separate things—and yet, it did. His mouth opened in a wordless cry, the agony too great to draw breath and scream.

"The dragons should have run with the rest of the fae rabble. Instead, they believed they could save everyone all by themselves.

Now here you are, at my feet." Harin's gloved fingers touched Ronan's cheek. Chill radiated from those fingertips, leaving him blessedly numb. "That's your first lesson about pride."

Harin snapped his fingers. This time, the aide stepped forward with something that gleamed in the sun. It was a lamp, which made no sense. Who needed light, when the sun beat down like a flame?

Harin took the lamp with the air of a showman performing tricks. "Now let me introduce you to lesson number two."

Present Day
The Human Realm.

Comfy Chair Books and Collectibles was not the natural habitat of a professional fighter, but that was where Barleycorn sent Alana. She soon discovered retail sales had all the adrenaline rush of lukewarm porridge.

She wasn't afraid of hard work, but the confinement irked her. She was used to jumping, running, and pushing her physical limits. Everything here was claustrophobic. The store was dark and cramped with floor-to-ceiling bookshelves, an impressive collection of dust and spiders, plus an occasional mouse. Still, it was a job with just enough pay to live on. All she had to do was show up and take money from the customers. It was a good-enough gig until she thought of something better.

A few weeks into her new career, a regular customer came in with a plastic bag of junk from a swap meet. Mr. Corby, the proprietor, bought the whole thing for cash. This was the collectibles part of Comfy Chair—a scattering of rotary-dial phones, tin soldiers, and ancient staplers graced the front area. Once the customer left counting his loot, Corby sorted through the bag's contents.

Alana leaned across the front desk. She wasn't that interested, but it was something to break up the interminable slog between lunch and quitting time. "Anything good?"

Corby was a squat demi-fae who appeared old enough to be her grandfather. Giving her a sharp look, he pulled a creepy doll out of the bag. "There are a couple of items we can put out front. The rest is garbage."

Alana eyed the doll, which—even to her poor magical sensors—gave off a whiff of unsavory magic. "What about that?"

"There's a collector who might be interested." He said it in a way that didn't invite more questions from the hired help. All the same, Alana had seen him stash items in his office safe before. He had a side hustle selling objects to select clients.

Alana folded her arms. "The guy who brought that in was human. He probably didn't know what he had."

Corby laughed—a rasping cackle. "Certain fae objects find their way into the outside world. Some humans recognize them as unique, but don't understand why."

"But they know they're valuable enough to sell to someone like you?"

"Indeed." He held the creepy doll up to the thin stream of light wavering through the dirty window, turning the ugly figure this way and that. "It's worth paying for a load of junk to pick out the one or two bits worth having."

"Then why not buy just those pieces?"

His smile was full of small yellow teeth. "Never let the customer know which are the gems, or they'll ask for more money."

"That doesn't seem fair," Alana pointed out.

"That's business. Buy low, sell high. I've no obligation to give free appraisals."

"But..."

"If an item has magical properties, it doesn't belong with humans. It's not just a waste; it could be dangerous."

Since Alana agreed with the last point, she let the subject drop. The school bell down the street had just signaled the end of the day, and now three boys came in searching for old graphic novels. Corby watched them in a way that said he knew exactly how much money was in their pockets, and he intended to get every cent. He oozed forward, hands clasped. "Can I help you young gentlemen find something?"

Alana slid off the stool behind the sales desk, then went into the back to refill her coffee mug. The perks of the job were few, but Corby kept a pot brewing most of the shift. She poured, deciding to take it black since the milk in the fridge was slowly turning to cheese.

A feeling of being watched prickled the back of her neck. She turned, glowering at the shadows. This part of the store was largely unfinished except for Corby's office and a workspace for unpacking and pricing books. The rest was bare floor stacked with overstock and bric-a-brac that hadn't quite made it to the garbage. She lifted her mug and sipped, still searching for whatever had set her nerves on edge. A rat? A ghost? A spell-book lost and discontented among the old thrillers? Whatever it was had to be strong, because subtle magic would sail right past her.

Her gaze slid to the open door of Corby's office. It was in there. She crossed the floor slowly, remembering she was never to set foot in her boss's personal space—as if anyone wanted to hang out in a broom closet that smelled like old pastrami. But then again, the safe was in there, with all the special goodies for his special customers.

She could feel the warding spell before she'd made it across the room. It didn't matter if the door was open—it was as good as locked and bolted. That didn't stop *something* from peering out at her. She paused just beyond the spell's reach, trying to see what was bugging her with the persistence of a hungry mosquito.

A flutter of excitement ran through Alana. Without the need to battle opponents, she'd relaxed her guard since coming to the store. That had been good for her healing body, but she'd grown restless. A touch of mystery—even just an odd feeling—made her come alive.

She took another swallow of strong coffee. Corby's desk held a lamp and a clutter of papers. She shifted to the left, but only saw the putty-colored corner of the wall safe. When she leaned to the right, there was an old mirror in a fancy frame. Nothing screamed sorcery—no wizard hats or magic wands. Not even a stray unicorn. Maybe this job was so mind-numbing she was making up threats to stay sane. Alana turned away just as Corby walked into the back.

"What are you doing back here?" he demanded.

"Getting coffee."

His brows lifted. "The coffee pot is on the other side of the room."

"I thought I heard something." It was almost true.

"You heard something that just so happens to be in the part of the premises that's none of your business?"

This sounded like an argument Alana wasn't about to win—not with words, at any rate. She moved to the counter, then set her coffee cup down. "I'm sorry. I'll get back to the front desk."

He didn't move from the doorway into the front of the store. He was much shorter than she was, but his sharp black eyes didn't waver from her face. Demi-fae were half human and mortal, but some were as powerful as any wizard. Alana guessed Corby was one of them.

"Stay out of my office."

"No problem," she said, but she knew a problem when it stared her in the face.

He still didn't move. "I'm leaving early today. I expect you to lock up. Don't think I won't know if you go snooping around."

Her temper bubbled, but she kept it contained. "Understood."

He finally stepped aside. Alana brushed past, shoulders rigid.

She was used to focusing her rage in a fight, but that wouldn't work here.

"Your job is to do what you're told," Corby called. "Don't think your pride matters to me."

No doubt that was true, but it wasn't uppermost in Alana's thoughts. All she could think about right then was how much she hated Barleycorn for giving her this job.

❀ 3 ❀

Blessedly, there were no customers. Once Alana got behind the counter, she balled her fists where Corby couldn't see her do it.

She concentrated on money.

She needed it for food, rent, and medicines.

Barleycorn never saw a job hunter twice.

This wasn't the time to walk out.

Maybe this was a cosmic test of her self-discipline.

It was all she could do not to scream.

She heard the office door slam, the sound carrying all the way from the back of the store. Then came the rattle as Corby turned the lock, underscoring his point that she was not welcome there. A moment later, he stumped past, crossing through the store and out the front door without so much as a glance her way. The instant he left, the air in the place felt lighter.

She took a deep breath, then let it out slowly. It would be hard to get another position—and harder still in the human world, where she couldn't explain her past. She was stuck at Comfy Chair, at least for a while.

Alana felt like a tigress trapped in a compact car.

The dregs of the afternoon dribbled away. Eventually, she began cashing out. Just as she was about to make a break for freedom, the door jangled. Reluctantly, she lifted her gaze to see a gray-haired woman with a paper box. With a dramatic sigh, the customer thumped her load down on the counter. "Thank heavens you're still open!"

Alana catalogued her: *human, late fifties, average in every obvious way*. "What can I do for you?"

"I heard through the grapevine that you buy collectibles."

And here Alana thought she'd be closing on time. "Once in a while."

"My aunt passed, and I'm clearing out her things. She was an odd duck, so there were some interesting pieces." The woman gave the box a significant glance.

Out of politeness, Alana lifted the flap and peeked inside. Most of the contents was kitchen clutter—a wall clock shaped like a tomato, cookie tins decorated with children and puppies and a device for making uniform hamburger patties. It was all about as magical as undercooked bread dough. She glanced up, seeing an almost painful hope in the woman's eyes. Maybe she needed money? "I can see what your aunt collected was very unique."

The woman brightened. "Really?"

"Sure." Alana picked up the stack of cash she'd been counting, then peeled off two bills. It wasn't a fortune, but still far too much for the junk. *Take that, Corby.* She thrust the money across the counter. "I'll buy the whole box."

The woman snatched the cash eagerly. "Thank you!"

"No problem. We'll see to it your aunt's things find excellent homes."

"Thank you," the woman said again with a gratitude that made Alana's stomach hurt.

She ushered the woman out the front door before locking it behind her. When the bolt slid home with a clack, Alana exhaled with relief. Another day at Comfy Chair over and done with.

She glanced at the box, thinking of all the people Corby had swindled out of their valuables. It served him right if she'd paid a premium price for rubbish. Plus, she'd made that woman's day. Win-win.

Suddenly, Alana was in a much better mood. Curious now, she unloaded the box onto the counter. There were baking pans, flowerpots with polka dots, and one of those cheap brass lamps that went in and out of fashion every two decades or so. It caught her eye because it had dragons on it, but her enthusiasm faded when the lid wouldn't come off. *Useless.* Still, it was the kind of fake exotic trinket that Tina had loved.

Tina. It was her birthday today. A wrench of sadness stole Alana's breath, almost doubling her over.

Quickly, she put everything back in the box and hauled it to a dark corner of the back room, then wrapped up the cash report. It had been a good day for business, despite her unauthorized purchase. When she was done, she made one final sale to herself.

Alana took the brass lamp, stuffing it into her tote bag.

When she went to visit Tina, she wouldn't go empty-handed.

BY THE TIME ALANA GOT OFF THE BUS AT THE GRAVEYARD, DUSK erased the edges of the afternoon shadows. The huge iron gates would be open for another hour, so she set off through the rows of yew and cedar, moving slowly to accommodate the pain of her ruined knee. A rising wind sang through the boughs. It was May, but she was grateful for her jacket.

The cemetery had a scattering of fae graves, but only a few. Full-blooded faeries didn't age, and demi-fae lived for centuries, so a demise from natural causes—even disease—was rare. However, they weren't indestructible. Bullets, blades, and poison could injure or kill them almost as readily as if they were mortal.

There was a small section in the northeast corner where fighters like Tina lay. Alana turned her steps toward them. Fae loved their blood sports, and unless death was possible, no game attracted high-rolling sponsors. All the same, fatalities weren't encouraged. Fighters were an investment. A corpse represented a waste of time and money.

And yet... as she reached the fae section of the graveyard, Alana read the names on the tombstones. There were three clustered together, the fresh white marble glowing in the fading light. Their cleanliness was a testament to how recent those deaths were—two other fighters, and then Tina. Alana knew them all, remembered their faces and families, the sounds of their laughter. After decades without such casualties, three were dead within a handful of years.

Something behind the scenes of the fights had changed. What was the saying? One was a misfortune, two a terrible coincidence, and three was... Alana couldn't remember the exact phrase. Suspicious? A pattern? Plainly criminal?

Alana had asked questions, but no one inside the games would answer. Competitors did what they were told if they wanted time in the ring, and they all wanted as many fights as they could get before injury forced them to retire. Visibility was the only way to keep their sponsors, their coaches, and most of all, their fans. Fighters were only as good as their last match, and memories were short. If they didn't grab every opportunity, the new kid on the block was quite happy to snatch it in their place.

Alana knelt before Tina's headstone, touching the dark earth with its stubble of new grass. Tears burned down her cheeks, as hot as the grave dirt was cold. They were both out of the game now, and Alana couldn't be swayed by promises of fame and fortune. She would find out why Tina had died. She could call out their betrayer. Make them pay.

The road to justice might be long, but an angry fae had nothing but time.

"Happy birthday, Paratina Meadow." Alana brought her friend's face to mind—her tumble of crazy hair, dancing black eyes, and that grin that promised havoc. Tina had been fierce—the archetype of a warrior—and she'd lived and breathed for the games. Just thinking about her, Alana smelled sawdust and resin and the scented oil they'd rubbed into their bruises. "I'll find out why this happened to you. I swear it."

Alana had made the vow before, the first time she'd come here, and she was no closer to an answer. Guilt dragged at her as she drew the lamp from her bag, wishing it were more than just a useless trinket. Still, it was pretty. The brass gleamed in the sun's dying rays, flaring on the wings of the embossed dragons. After wiping the dust away from the lamp with the sleeve of her jacket, she set it before Tina's headstone. Yes, it was just the sort of tacky, shiny clutter that Tina had loved. It wasn't much, but the affection that went with it was real.

The light was all but gone, dusk claiming the sky. Alana rose, the rising dampness stiffening her battered joints. It was time to go home to her tiny apartment—make ready for another fascinating day as Corby's wage slave. But as she slung her bag over her shoulder, she took a second look at the lamp. It seemed to be...glowing?

A faint tingling coursed up her arms, hot and cold at once. She fell back a step, clenching her teeth against the sensation. Panic rose like a half-formed shout. As if to spite her, the glow pulsed brighter and brighter, casting sharp-edged shadows with its ruddy light. All at once, the lamp belched a cloud of smoke like a bad stage effect. She took another step back, expecting to choke, but the smoke had no scent as it rose and swirled into a tall plume.

The impulse to run sang through her. She hadn't felt a lick of power in that lamp before now. Her magical senses were weak, but she should have felt something—unless this was top-drawer sorcery, with a load of fancy shielding magic. But then, what would it be doing in a box of kitchen collectibles?

Despite her alarm, curiosity glued her feet to the ground. She'd seen plenty of magic in her day, but this was something new. As the cloud of smoke condensed, the glow faded like a dying ember. Alana narrowed her eyes, trying to judge when she could safely stuff the lamp back into her bag and run before a groundskeeper showed up to investigate the unexpected light. Except...

The column of smoke grew thicker and paler, until a form began to emerge—muscular limbs, a face, and then a leather tunic sewn with dark, overlapping metal scales. Armor, Alana guessed, but a style that had gone out of fashion along with spears and chariots. Spooked, she scrambled to a respectful distance.

The man materializing before her was tall, extraordinarily so, with collar-length dark hair. He was an experienced warrior—that much was plain from the way he stood, feet apart and weight balanced as if ready to leap into action. He carried no weapons, but something said he didn't need them. Those large hands, arms roped with muscle, could easily take care of business. He tilted his head, considering her with eyes dark as obsidian. Everything about him screamed fae—one with a depth of power she'd never seen before.

Then he swept a low bow, one hand rising to cover his heart. "Your wish is my command, mistress."

Alana's mouth fell open. "Say that again?"

Impatience flashed in his eyes. "Your wish. My command."

"Okay..." She wondered if she looked that way when a customer asked a stupid question. "Who are you, and what were you doing in my lamp?"

"I am Ronan. I am here to serve."

"And the lamp?"

"Is my...home." His expression was carefully blank.

"That must suck." She didn't know what else to say. "I'm Alana."

He bowed again, showing off the easy grace of a leopard. "Mistress Alana, I am your servant."

Alana thought of the many times she'd daydreamed about a strapping man slave groveling at her feet, but this was beyond weird. "So why are you here?"

He straightened, clasping his hands behind his back and lifting his chin. "When a fae takes possession of the lamp, Mistress Alana, I am obligated to grant that fae three wishes."

"I could wish for anything?"

His jaw bunched, as if he ground his teeth. "Any wishes you desire."

Inevitably, she thought of the obvious—health, fortune, and fame. Most of all, that the fatal fight had never happened. "Nothing that good comes without a price."

He closed the distance between them with one long stride. Alana's insides tightened. She was used to holding her own against any male, but he towered over her. He wasn't just big; he had presence. Every plane of his face was sharply sculpted. His nose was blade straight and his mouth generous. Right now, his deep-set eyes were intent on her face, and she had to fight not to squirm.

"There is no trick," he said. "It is simply what I say. Three wishes. Not two. Not four. Three and only three."

"Three lightning bolts of absolute power," she murmured, still a prisoner of those eyes. "You can do that?"

"I can." His smile showed even white teeth, but it didn't go beyond his mouth.

Perhaps it was because she was still caught in the misery of her workday, but there was something familiar in his determined courtesy. "You're obligated to grant me three moments of complete command over the universe, yet you're stuck in a brass lamp at the end of the day?"

He folded his arms. "I am the servant of the lamp."

Alana didn't understand what was going on, but something

about this chilled her to the bone. She turned away. "I don't want your wishes."

He caught her arm, gently but firmly drawing her back to face him. "But you do. I can taste them on the air. You want your friend back. You want to fight again. Most of all, you want to punish whomever betrayed you."

Alana stared. "Get out of my head."

"I've named three wishes right there," he said quietly. "Take them. That's what I'm here for."

It was oh so tempting—especially with Ronan so close. Whatever else he might be, he was a healthy male, the heat of his body a persuasion all on its own. She'd been alone too long, and she began to wish for things she hoped he couldn't detect.

Still—she wasn't stupid. "No thanks."

She pulled out of his grasp. His eyes widened a moment, but whether that was from anger or surprise, she couldn't tell.

"Don't be foolish. Your body cries out to be healed." His hand made a stroking gesture before her, not quite touching but close enough she felt the movement of air. His long fingers seemed to pinch together as he swept his arm from her head to her feet, catching something imaginary and tossing it aside.

Or not so imaginary. Alana felt suddenly exposed, but her clothes were still there. Despite herself, she touched her arms, her stomach, seeking for soreness that simply wasn't there. A web of weakness had been drawn away. She inhaled, testing her body.

Strength surged back as if a dam had burst. The slow breath turned into a gasp as she skittered backward in shock. Unbidden tears clogged her throat when her joints responded, elastic and free of pain.

Then she sobered suddenly, her joy sliced short as she recalled she had no idea what she was dealing with. "How did you do that?"

He waved his hands in an exasperated gesture. "I am a genie, a jinn, the genius of the lamp. Power is mine to command."

She bit her lip. "I said I didn't want any wishes."

Ronan's mouth quirked. It was the first sign of a real response she'd seen from him. "Consider that a free taste of what is possible, Mistress Alana."

He'd taken her refusal as a challenge, a gauntlet thrown down. His response awakened her own competitive nature. What sort of a battle could he provide? She could feel temptation stir, both for this handsome creature *and* what he offered. If he could take her pain so easily, what else could he do?

He touched her sleeve. "I can take my healing one step further. You have scars I can smooth away. It is no trouble at all, for a woman so lovely as you. You just have to wish it."

"No!" She pushed his hand aside. "Those are mine. I earned them all."

They were evidence of who she was and where she'd been. Of the lessons she'd learned and the battles she'd won. They were reminders of how hard she'd fought the night Tina had given her life. She wasn't about to treat her scars with shame.

Ronan narrowed his eyes, annoyance hardening his features. "Then what use am I to you, mistress, if you despise everything I have to give?"

Alana angrily stepped back. "You call me mistress? Then I command you to get back in your lamp and leave me alone!"

❧   4   ❧

othingness.

Alana had barely finished talking when Ronan's perceptions vanished. Inside the lamp, he hovered without sight or touch or sense of time in an endless, unrelieved void. Still, he was aware. Ronan always knew who possessed the lamp—and him.

There had been hundreds, perhaps thousands, since Harin Blacktongue had enslaved him. At first, they had been those Harin or his master, the King of Shades, wished to befriend—or ensnare. Emperors. Potentates. Queens. The wishes of the powerful had been colorful, grand, and often bloody. But then the lamp had been carried to the human realm, and passed from hand to hand. Requests from the exiled fae became simpler, but no less profound. Love. Vengeance. The need to measure up. Always in the end, despair. Wishes were meant to be simply that—butterflies of unfocused desire. They were never designed to fill the heart.

Ronan heard it all, over and over and over. He began in a state of sorrow, pitying every foolish choice. Forced to grovel and grant each one. No one with power over the universe—however brief—listened to good advice. It was like watching the same carriage accident a thousand times. Nothing he did changed a thing. Now he swung between apathy and rage. Eventually, he would go mad.

Except something new had happened. No one had ever refused his wishes before. That had revived an emotion he'd all but forgotten—curiosity. It rushed through him like a cold salt wave, jolting him awake.

He was also attuned to his owner's state of mind. This woman, Alana, was shocked he had disappeared back into his prison. After she had snatched up the lamp, she had run from the graveyard. Beyond that, there was a jumble of images, mostly of the inside of her cluttered shoulder bag.

Who was his new mistress? When he'd healed her, he'd become aware she was as strong as any warrior. Her limbs were slight but sleek with muscle. Such battle-hardened women had existed in the long-ago days of his freedom, but they were uncommon.

Then again, nothing about this Alana was usual. She was beautiful, her features delicate like the woodland fae, with a pointed chin and hair pale as the first sunlight of spring. For a wild, bestial instant, he'd wanted to lay her down on the soft, dew-laden grass. Yes, it was a cemetery, but he'd been imprisoned in a lamp for a very long time.

Eventually, he felt his prison turning around and around as if Alana were examining it from all angles. Although he had no real sense of direction, the motion made him dizzy. Irritated, Ronan wafted out of the lamp and materialized with folded arms. "You summoned me?"

"Hi," she said, clutching the lamp with a guilty expression. "How does this thing work?"

"Beginners," he muttered under his breath.

"What's that?"

He forced a smile to his lips. "A light polish will do."

"You mean rubbing?" Her forehead wrinkled. "That seems—kinda inappropriate."

He wondered if he were capable of headaches. "I am not responsible for the design."

"Okay." She set the lamp down, then wiped her palms on her jeans. "Have a seat. We need to talk."

Ronan hesitated, uneasiness seeping through him. He'd explained the wishes. He had nothing else to offer. "What is there to discuss?"

"How did your lamp end up in a box of junk?" she asked.

"By chance, I was lost among mortal households for a time. Humans do not have the power to summon me."

"So you got a break?"

"I remained inactive in the lamp for a year or two."

She studied him, her frank gaze roving over his features. He felt a boyish urge to fidget under the scrutiny. Few ever looked at a genie in any detail, much less *saw* them. If he ever returned to his old life, Ronan would never look past his servants again. Now he understood that the boy who held his horse and the man who tended his garden had lives and loves and needs of their own. Ronan turned away from Alana, afraid to remember too much. It was better to keep memories locked away where they couldn't torment him.

He finally took notice of where they were. A room with a wooden floor, plain white walls, and functional furniture. Alana sat at a pine table next to a kitchen nook. Her bed was in the opposite corner. The view through the windows showed a scatter of lights. He guessed that such lights meant he was looking out over a city. "Is this your home, mistress?"

"My apartment. I've not been here long. I had to move to a studio space I could afford."

Some of the terms were strange to him, but he could tell there was a story in what she said. An old part of him wanted to hear it and help if he could. As a prince of the land, he was bred to look after his people.

On the other hand, he'd rather not know a thing about this woman. In his transformation from dragon to genie, he had gained enormous magical power but lost much freedom. As the servant of the lamp, he *had* to grant three wishes—any three wishes, however misguided or horrific—and move on. The curse allowed nothing else.

"Please sit down," Alana repeated. "And please don't call me mistress. It makes you sound like a butler."

Obediently, he sat in the chair opposite hers, the table between them. "As you command." All right, so he was still capable of understated sarcasm.

She put her chin in her hand, pursing her lips in thought. Ronan found himself drawn to their plump, perfect bow.

"Does a command count as a wish?" she asked.

"No." He moved his attention to her clear gray eyes. They were no less distracting than her lips, so he studied the calendar on the wall. He had no business ogling the woman. "Wishes are specific and important to the one doing the wishing."

"Like what?"

"Love. Fortune. Death. Vengeance." He waved a dismissive hand. "A dream vacation. Things beyond normal reach."

"But only three of them."

"True." What he could not say was that no owner of the lamp had ever been satisfied with three. They always wanted more, and more, and more. That had brought all those emperors and queens to grovel at Harin's feet. It was what made the lamp a weapon. Even with Harin in one realm and Ronan in another, the curse still held. Sooner or later, everyone the lamp—and Ronan— touched became corrupt. Even this woman, eventually.

She sat back. "What do you get out of this?"

If only she would start wishing so he could move on to someone less... uncomfortable. Most would be crowing about all the marvelous things they'd achieve with a genie in their pocket. She wasn't. How was he supposed to do his job?

"You are a bizarre woman."

"My name is Alana."

He knew that, but had chosen to avoid the feel of it on his tongue. She would be hard enough to forget without tasting her name every time he spoke.

She chewed her lip. "You don't like to talk, do you?"

"No." Her questions forced him to look inward, and he was terrified he'd find nothing left. "I grant wishes because I must. That is my function. There is no more to explain."

And yet, he didn't want the strange moment to end. He hadn't had a conversation of any kind since, well, he couldn't remember, but top hats had been in fashion.

"Were you always this grumpy?" she asked.

"I don't know. Why don't you want your wishes?"

"Maybe I don't know the best way to get what I want." She gave him a narrow look. "Maybe I want to read the fine print."

"Do you think I'm lying?"

"I'm a fighter, and I'm a fae. I know I won't get something for nothing, and maybe I want to test your defenses first." She shrugged. "And you worry me."

"How?"

"You remind me of a big, beaten dog. I don't know if you're savage, in trouble, or both."

His breath hitched at the words. They were far too just. "I can't harm you. I am your slave."

"Did I force you to go back into your lamp?"

"Yes."

"Does that bother you?"

It wasn't the question he'd expected. "No one likes to be forced."

"I'm sorry." She put her hand over his. "I didn't mean to be rude."

He froze, fixated by the feel of her hand over his. Slowly, he forced his gaze down to see his sun-darkened skin covered by her pale fingers. Her hand was elegantly proportioned, but it was covered by the tiny scars one got by handling edged weapons. Yes, indeed, her scars were part of who she was.

That same hand was offering him comfort. What a strange, strange woman. He slid away from her touch, unsettled. Kindness was a gift he could not use. He would forget this as soon as possible. "Perhaps I can help you with your wishes."

"How?" she asked, sitting back in her chair and withdrawing the hand she had extended.

He suddenly realized he would do anything to make her reach out again.

"Tell me why you want vengeance for your friend."

THE NEXT DAY, ALANA STOOD BEHIND THE SALES DESK AT Comfy Chair, fighting to stay awake after talking with Ronan most of the night. She'd begun the conversation uncertain if she should feed him, kiss him, or chain him up. Most of her energy had been spent trying to figure out the whole genie situation, and why anyone hung out in a lighting fixture doling out instant gratification. However, whenever she got close to an answer, Ronan clammed up. By the end of the night, he was dialing down the surliness, but they had a long way to go before she gave him an ounce of trust. For all that he was devastatingly good-looking, she was frustrated enough to break something over his head.

She wasn't making wishes anytime soon. Not until she knew what was going on.

Now it was Saturday, the shop's busiest day of the week, and there had been a steady stream of customers. The downside was that she desperately wanted to mull over the Ronan factor. The upside was that so far, there'd been no time for Corby to resume his foul mood. If he'd noticed the box of kitchen collectibles she'd bought the night before, he'd said nothing about it.

She'd left the lamp at home. Since it was exactly the sort of thing Corby sold to his clients, she figured it was better keeping it off his radar. When she'd left for work, Ronan had been staring out the window at the horizon, mesmerized by the seaplanes that flew in and out of the harbor.

She took cash from a young man buying a tattered sword and sorcery paperback before sending him on his way. Then came a regular who bought a stack of romance novels at least once a week. As she rang them through, Alana picked up the top one to read the back.

"A prince takes a vow of silence until his lady love agrees to marry him," she read aloud.

"I think I'll leave it around for my husband," the woman said dryly. "Maybe he'll take the hint about giving me some peace and quiet."

Alana laughed and counted out change, giving the customer a price break because she was a frequent flyer. When Alana looked up next, there wasn't anyone else waiting. They'd come to a lull in the Saturday rush.

Corby wandered over. He hit the button on the till that showed the sales so far, grunting in satisfaction at the total. "A good morning."

"I'll go restock the fantasy display. It got picked clean." Alana hurried away, not wanting any more conversation with her boss than was strictly required.

She was halfway across the store when he spoke. "Have you been doing exercises or something?"

She turned back in confusion. "Why?"

"You're not limping so much."

She tried to read his expression, imagining his pointed nose sniffing out the fact she'd been healed. That would only lead to awkward questions. "I guess I am getting a bit better."

She turned away, slowing her movements down so she didn't appear overly energetic. Her mind churned as she worked. If she didn't want Ronan's wishes, why not return the lamp to the store and let Corby sell it to one of his customers?

Every instinct screamed not to do it. Even if Corby was grateful—she couldn't picture that, but whatever—she wasn't sure she wanted the lamp in just anyone's hands. The whole three-wishes thing seemed fishy. Plus, there was Ronan himself to consider. He deserved some say in the matter.

One of the paperbacks was losing its cover, so she returned to the desk in search of mending tape. "I have a question," she said to Corby. "I know you don't buy every bag and box of collectibles that come in here. How do you know which ones are good?"

Corby frowned. "We're back to that, are we?"

Alana didn't meet his eyes, but concentrated on taping the book back together. "I honestly want to know."

"It's my talent," he said brusquely. "I have a nose for faery workmanship."

"There seems to be a lot in circulation, given what shows up here."

"A lot came with us when we escaped the old world." He shrugged. "Quite a bit got sold or traded to the humans as the fae settled here."

"I wonder how long it's been since some of these things have been in fae hands," she mused. Corby's explanation fit with what Ronan had said about the lamp ending up lost among the mortals.

"That's one reason why I keep an eye out for items with fae origins," Corby said. "Like I said, some of them aren't safe."

Just then, the door opened. Corby's attention snapped to the man who entered. "Mr. Martigen!"

Alana raised her head to see—and her brain stalled. The guy was incredibly good-looking—tall, young, well-built, and wearing a suit that had to cost as much as the entire store. She stood straight, responding to his charismatic smile. With fair hair and cornflower-blue eyes, he reminded her of a prince from a bedtime story. This was Tyrell Martigen, heir to the aristocratic fae family that ran Martigen Industries—and Martigen Industries was a big sponsor of the underground fights.

"Corby." Martigen sailed past Alana without glancing her way. "You have something for me? I don't have much time."

Alana bristled. She'd earned him enough money that he should have spared her a moment. Nonetheless, Martigen headed for the back without breaking stride. Corby fell into step behind him like an obedient dog.

Clearly, this wasn't the man's first visit to Corby's treasure vault.

❧   5   ❧

Alana took a swallow from her coffee mug as the two men vanished into the back. She looked up when the door chimed, almost resentful that a customer had interrupted her brooding. Then she nearly choked on her coffee. Ronan strode into the shop, but not the Ronan she'd seen just hours ago. He'd lost the armor. His long legs sported tight denim, and a T-shirt strained across his broad chest. His hair was wet, probably from a shower, and curling against the nape of his neck. Alana's world tilted as half-remembered needs flared low in her belly. With a cough, she slammed her mug to the counter. Was her mouth actually watering?

There were bigger problems than her libido. Her genie from the lamp was on the loose, and he'd apparently gone shopping. "What are you doing here?" she demanded, none too gently. "How did you even find me?"

His expression was just shy of an eye roll. "I belong to you. For now at least."

"Okay, fine. Where did you get the clothes?"

"Don't you like them? I chose something that seems to be common wear among your people." He leaned against one of the tall bookcases, folding his arms. His air had the practiced negligence of an underwear model, but his eyes burned with that same resentful fury she'd seen before.

"Your outfit is fine, but..."

"If you prefer..." He made a circling gesture with one hand. He was suddenly wearing full Highland gear, complete with a kilt and feathered bonnet. Something in his double-dog-dare expression said there was nothing under that scrap of plaid.

Alana blinked, giving herself a mental cold shower. She should have seen this coming. He was a genie, after all. He could a show up as a puppy, a llama, or a teapot if he wanted to. That was just plain logic.

A less rational part of her brain really liked the Scottish look, but that would raise questions. Questions were bad. "Um, very nice, but I don't think..."

Another hand wave, and he was wearing a form-fitting tux, complete with white tie. *Yowzah!* James Bond with all the trimmings. Alana took a deep breath, summoning what little self-discipline she had left. "Please go back to the first option."

With a semi-sarcastic nod, Ronan returned to casual dress. Alana leaned forward, bracing her elbows on the counter. "Seriously," she said, lowering her voice. "What are you doing here? It could be dangerous. There's a vault in the back for, um, stray magical items."

Ronan's mouth quirked. "How nice to be classified as lost and found."

Alana grimaced and opened her mouth to reply, but Ronan held up a hand.

"Who's that?" he asked, his own voice soft.

Alana listened. It was Corby's voice drifting from the back room, raised in a tone she knew all too well. He was frustrated and losing his temper. "For the last time," her boss said, "I *have* been looking for it. I've set every spell in the book to draw it my way."

"Well, it isn't working," Martigen replied.

"It is. At least, the attraction spells are strong enough. You wouldn't believe the piles of crap I've had to sort through, but every fae-made knickknack in the city is coming through the doors."

That answered Alana's question about how Corby got his hands on so many enchanted items. It really was his special magical talent.

"But you haven't found the one we *need*," Martigen shot back.

"I need it, too!"

"The company needs it more!"

Martigen's tone sawed Alana's nerves. He was more than a disappointed collector—for some reason, he was desperate.

"What's the matter?" Corby replied, sarcasm thick in his voice. "The board of directors needs a wish granted?"

Ronan's head lifted. They were singing his song.

"Who doesn't need that?" Martigen asked in an acerbic tone. "But it's our investor who wants it, and none of us is in a position to deny him."

Corby grunted, a mix of disgust and resignation.

Ronan met Alana's eyes, and she saw her own thoughts reflected there. Tyrell Martigen was clearly hunting for the lamp —to give to his investor. Who was that?

Martigen Enterprises made money as bookmakers, but their main income came from the human stock market. They were clearly profitable, so why did they need an investor? And if the investor knew about the lamp, he knew about the fae, so...

Her mind spun, trying to put the pieces together. She remembered the guy—Randall—she'd met just before her interview with Barleycorn. He'd been waiting for an interview with the family. Why were they hiring? Maybe there was no connection, but...

She had a sudden conviction they had to leave before Corby and Martigen returned from the back. Wasting no time, she grabbed the sign on the door and turned it around so the "closed" side was out. "Let's go."

Ronan raised an eyebrow.

"I'm entitled to a lunch break," she replied. "And you're coming."

"Of course," he said dryly. "I live to obey."

A flash of irritation made her grab a fistful of his T-shirt and propel him toward the door. She released him once they were on the pavement, trying to ignore the body warmth that clung to her hand. She turned to lock the door, then gave him a shove toward the restaurant on the corner. He looked over his shoulder, a hint of amusement in his face, as if her attempts at physical control were laughable. Alana gritted her teeth, pretending not to notice.

"Do you mind Italian?" she asked.

"In what way?"

"In a fettuccini way."

"I do not require food."

"I didn't ask if you required it. Do you eat?"

"I am capable."

"Then join me." It came out in a growl. The thought of not needing to eat—it said more than anything else about how he was trapped, suspended in some in-between state, not really alive and not quite—whatever. She didn't want to think about it too closely. Something told her pity was the last thing he wanted.

The place was a tiny, family run affair that had a menu almost as small as their premises. Mama Taglioni wrote the menu on the chalkboard every morning. She was also prone to emerging from the kitchen to chat, check out the newcomers, and generally rule over her oregano-scented domain. The eatery was the neighborhood's kitchen away from home.

Despite the steady stream of regulars, Alana always managed to find room at one of the two-seater wooden tables that lined the walls. She suspected it was because Mama had made her a personal project, down to subscribing a home remedy for her aching muscles. Of course, her injuries hadn't so much as twinged since Ronan had healed her. She would find a way to thank him, somehow.

They took a seat in the back, out of sight of the windows. Alana and Ronan both went for the seat facing the door, but she got there first. He settled slowly as Maria, the daughter of the formidable Mama, came over with menus. She cast an appraising glance at Ronan, her lips parting slightly as she got an eyeful of his handsome dark features.

"Two specials," Alana said before the waitress settled in for a serious flirtation. She'd seen the girl with other patrons, and was stopping that show before it started. For some absurd reason, she felt protective of the genie, at least where Maria was concerned.

Maria left with one meaningful sidelong perusal of Ronan, who seemed oblivious. He was staring out at the street, his long-fingered hands drumming a complicated rhythm on the wooden tabletop.

"What are you thinking?" Alana asked.

When he turned, the sun caught his features, sculpting them with stark light and shadow. "Let me ask rather what you were thinking when you rushed us out of the bookstore."

She shrugged. "I was worried Corby would recognize you."

"He does not know me."

"He would know you're magical. That's his talent."

"Perhaps," Ronan agreed. "And your concern is charming. What else were you thinking?"

She straightened the container of paper napkins, lining them up with the salt and pepper. Nerves made her fidget. "Martigen. How would they know about your lamp?"

Ronan's hands stilled their drum solo and his expression grew thoughtful, for once devoid of resentment. "No one seeks the lamp for a good purpose."

It wasn't an answer, but it was revealing. "Why not? Who wouldn't want to get their hands on you?"

His eyebrows lifted. "You, apparently."

Their lunch arrived, Maria lingering a little too long before she sashayed back to the kitchen. Alana scowled, but it was hard to hang onto dark thoughts. Steam arose from the plates of pasta, richly scented with garlic. It was like a potion for contentment.

She dug in, gesturing for Ronan to do the same. He took a forkful, tasting it slowly. She watched the expressions dance across his face—caution, surprise, and then pleasure. His second bite was hearty, his third following along without delay.

"Doesn't anyone feed you?" Alana asked incredulously.

He swallowed, running his tongue along his teeth. "Not until they want something I cannot easily give."

"You need a union." She chewed, briefly closing her eyes to better taste the spices before regarding him once more.

His face had gone carefully neutral, back to the blankness she'd first seen from him. It was only then she realized how much of himself he'd shown her.

She reached out, putting a hand on his wrist. "I'm sorry."

Confusion flickered across his features, but then he went back to business. "If Martigen is required to find my lamp, his investor is in deep with the worst of villains."

Alana blinked, surprised by the fact he'd volunteered information. "What do you mean?"

Ronan set down his fork. "I'm a weapon, not a curiosity."

Alana quirked a brow. "Explain that."

He sat back. "There are things I cannot explain."

"Try harder."

Something like dismay flashed behind his eyes, but whatever he might have said was interrupted by the cannonball form of Mama Taglioni bustling up to the table. She cast a calculating glance at Ronan, then at Alana. "So who is this you bring to my kitchen, Alana?"

By her tone, she might as well have asked if they were engaged. Then her eyebrows went up as she spotted the half-eaten pasta. Alana watched in fascination as Mama put one finger under Ronan's chin and turned his face to hers. "You do not eat all my food?"

Unbelievably, a wide grin split Ronan's face. It was like heavy curtains parting on a cloudless noon sky. Alana hid her stunned reaction behind a bite of pasta.

Ronan rose, his tall frame towering over the woman. He took her weathered hands in his and—Alana's eyes bulged—bowed low in a gesture of respect. "On the contrary, I treasure the welcome that flows through your meal. If I am slow to finish, it is merely because of my captivating company."

Mama Taglioni's round face turned pink. The princely response—there was no other word for it—had charmed her down to her orthopedic soles. "Ah, yes, our Alana has eaten here alone far too many times."

"I'm never alone," Alana said defensively. "We're all family here."

Yes, she had far more in common with a hard-working human family than she did with the genie. Whoever he'd been in his pre-lamp days, he'd been schooled in the social graces, and that meant wealth and rank. Under any other circumstances, Alana would have been beneath his notice. It made the thought of them as a couple ridiculous.

She almost cringed when Mama gave her cheek a motherly tap. "Of course you're family, dear, always," their hostess said. "Though it's nice to see you bring a friend. Eat up, but save room for dessert."

"Dessert?" Ronan asked with the first spark of eagerness Alana had seen.

Mama laughed, giving his broad shoulder a squeeze. "The first of the strawberries are in," she said, then launched into a catalogue of ice cream, pies, and cream pastries. Just listening made Alana feel fat. It earned Mama another of Ronan's heart-stopping grins.

"We will do the selection justice," Ronan promised, somehow closing the conversation without sounding as if he were doing so. More of those upper-crust skills Alana had never mastered.

After that, Mama left them alone. Ronan leaned across the table. "Returning to our previous conversation, you learned a few of Corby's secrets this afternoon—he is a dealer caught in Martigen's web. You need to find your answers at a level above him. Learn what Martigen is involved in."

"How?" Although she knew the answer as soon as she spoke. She'd originally intended to work as a bodyguard for some young shark like Tyrell Martigen.

Ronan's gaze searched her face. "You have an idea."

Alana shook her head. "Barleycorn got me the job with Corby. He never sees a client twice, and he pretty much handles all the employment contracts in the fae community. If I leave and need a job again, I'm on my own and not likely to survive."

"Barleycorn..." Ronan repeated the name slowly. "I know him of old. John Barleycorn can be a formidable ally, but also a fox among the fowl."

"I want answers," Alana said, slumping in her chair. She had to know why Tina was poisoned, and who'd done it. If she worked for Tyrell Martigen, she'd be near the fighting scene again. It wasn't a direct route to finding her betrayer, but it was as good as she could hope for. At the same time...

"You are afraid to risk Barleycorn's displeasure," Ronan guessed.

"Maybe I'm overestimating what I can do. I'm not a trained investigator." She chewed a mouthful of cooling pasta. It might as well have been cardboard, for all she tasted it.

"Have faith. You are battle hardened, and you know the fighting business." Ronan smiled, but this time it was rueful. She hadn't earned the grin he'd given Mama Taglioni. "Experience and knowledge are more than most get in their moment of crisis."

Alana imagined herself working as Tyrell Martigen's protector.

A flutter of anticipation reminded her how most women would relish the idea of guarding his lean and sculpted body. At the same time, he—or at least his family—was at the heart of the deception that ended with Tina's death. Either way, it was a hazardous path.

A path she had to take. Otherwise, the fact she'd survived the fight meant nothing. "I'll do it. I don't know how, but I'll find a way."

Ronan sat back, his face a shade paler than before. "You could use a wish. You have three."

Alana pushed her plate away. "No. This is my fight. I'll do it myself."

"I could help you. You don't need to do this alone."

"I am alone."

Ronan raised a brow. "We'll see. Now, how about dessert?"

❧ 6 ❧

After their meal was over, Alana returned to the store to finish her shift. Ronan explored the town alone, his stomach full for the first time since—he didn't know. Time had no meaning inside the lamp. All that mattered right now was that someone had seen to his needs.

The repast had fed more than his body. Once upon a time, he would have scorned such simple fare, for a dinner with seven or eight courses was standard at his father's court. But the matron who had cooked his meal, with her rough hands and food-stained apron, had looked upon him with concern for his comfort. When had that happened last?

And what of Alana? She had taken him there—pushing and pulling like an impatient shepherdess—to keep him safe. She wasn't magically powerful—she'd barely been fae enough to summon him in the first place—yet she'd done what she could. No one had tried to protect him since he was a boy learning to toddle. He had been Prince Ronan of Bright Wing, the one born to safeguard his people—not the other way around.

Being looked after for a change was, in a word, amazing. Gratitude was a meager term for the storm of feeling inside him. This was a lesson the lamp had taught him. Oh, he had been grateful before—his parents had taken care to raise their children well. But they had been royalty, and they had the best and the most. There were so many simple gifts he would never have noticed as a prince. The freedom to choose his own comings and goings. To be seen as a person, not just a provider. A hand over his own.

Escaping the relentless solitude of the lamp was almost as good. He wandered through the downtown, marveling at the tall buildings and the rushing crowds. He'd seen cities like this over the centuries, each one bigger and busier than the last. He liked the excitement of them, the noisy bustle and raw vitality that swept him along the streets. For a moment, he belonged to the world again, even if it wasn't his own.

Ronan arrived at his destination, which was the street corner opposite Comfy Chair. There was a coffee shop there. If he took a seat at one of the tables, he could watch the bookstore's doorway without being seen. The waitress brought his order in a plain white mug. Ronan sniffed and then took a sip, wincing a little at the bitterness. Coffee was an acquired taste, and he'd only had a few opportunities to try it.

Which begged the question of why, when he had so few chances to roam free, was he spending his time watching Alana's workplace like a dog moping for his owner's return? Frowning, Ronan set the mug down. He was compelled to offer wishes, but he didn't have a time limit. He could take a day off.

He scratched his chin, feeling the beginnings of stubble. It felt strange. He was rarely out of the lamp long enough to need a shave—and maybe that was why he was here. All this unprecedented freedom had him off balance. Alana's kindness made him anxious to reciprocate. It had been too long since he'd shared in the give and take that wove relationships. So here he was, watching out for her interests. He knew the Martigen family from before the war, and he wondered what nonsense they were up to now.

The door to Comfy Chair swung open, and Tyrell emerged. Whatever he'd been discussing with Corby, it had been a long conversation. Since Ronan himself was one of the topics, that wasn't reassuring. He watched the man saunter down the street, his hands in his pockets and his head held high. The thought of Alana—cool, strong, beautiful, and lithe—guarding the young idiot rankled. Would she try to comfort him, too? Would she put her hand over his as well? If Martigen overstepped the line...

Ronan leashed his imagination, stopping it cold. He'd do best to focus on what he, a genie with virtually no freedom, could realistically achieve. Well, Alana had dragged him off and fed him lunch, so the least he could do was see if Tyrell Martigen was likely to get his bodyguards killed. Given the players involved in this drama so far, that was a distinct possibility. He pushed back his chair, stood, and left his half-drunk coffee to go cold. With a flick of his fingers, he conjured human money from Tyrell's wallet and left it for the waitress, including a generous tip.

Ronan slipped out of the café and fell into step behind Martigen, determined to find answers.

No sooner had Martigen left the back room of the bookstore than Corby emerged, stomped past Alana, and then took off down the street in the opposite direction from Tyrell. Whatever had passed between the two men, Alana was certain Corby had been the loser.

The murmur of voices coming from behind Corby's office door had been low and intense—which made it hard to eavesdrop once she got back from lunch. Not that the two men had paid any attention to her comings and goings. She doubted they would have noticed a parade of dancing trolls, they'd been so wrapped up in their debate.

Left alone in the store, she hitched herself onto the counter, swinging her feet as she puzzled over what to do. Did she really want to work for Tyrell? How would Corby react? Would it really get her any closer to finding out what really happened the night Tina was killed?

Alana had been over her last fight a hundred times. What she remembered first was the dry sensation in her mouth, as if sand coated her tongue all the way down her throat. That was her fear response. Others got twitchy or went to the bathroom a dozen times before a match. She got a thirst nothing could cure.

That night, her dry mouth was worse than ever because it was the finals. Alana and Tina—known to the world as the Incorruptible and the Indestructible—were set to fight the Slash, two cat shifters who had sprung on the scene that season and literally clawed their way to the top. The betting was astronomical, and it had gone in favor of Alana's team. The hopes and dreams of fans and gamblers alike rode on her will to win.

Alana stood in her place by the fighting circle, Henry to her right and Tina carrying on with an impromptu entourage. The battleground was really just a chalk dust circle on the sand floor of an underground arena. Bleachers circled it, with balcony boxes for the officials and wealthy patrons. The rank and file sat on the bare wood. If they had wings, they fluttered above the throng. The air smelled of nervous sweat and the honey wine favored by the fae.

Alana checked the buckles of her leather body armor for the fifth time, fingers clumsy with nerves. Henry handed her the water bottle, demonstrating how well he knew her. Alana rinsed her mouth, wishing it would ease her throat.

"Remember to stop telegraphing with your left foot," Henry reminded her. "And keep your eyes up. If the dirt's telling you something, it's because you're about to kiss it."

He'd put them through their paces hard that week, leaving nothing to chance. Alana was good, but Tina moved like a molten blade, brilliant and lethal. She was indestructible because she was impossibly fast.

Alana glanced at her partner, who in turn was making a rude gesture at the Slash. Their opponents fought half-shifted, upright but furry. Alana had always liked kitties, but this was enough to turn her against pets for good. The big one was staring across the circle with a sharp-toothed grin.

Just one more thing to make Alana jittery that day. She'd rolled out of bed with an unexpected chill in her belly. The air was rife with an electricity that stirred the hair along her arms. Something wasn't right.

"We need to call this off." The words came out of Alana's mouth unbidden.

Henry stared at her in bewilderment—as if she'd suddenly turned into a giraffe. "What?"

Her heart thundered. "There's something off about this fight. Don't ask me what it is because I don't know, but it's there."

Henry snorted. "What you're feeling is normal, kid. You've never been in a fight this big."

He was right about that. They'd had to post guards on their workout rooms to keep the curious away. All the same, no practice went without pictures appearing online—Tina in a spin kick, Alana punching a bag, their sparring partners flat on their backs. The upcoming battle was their few minutes of fame among the fae.

"Maybe, but I'm serious."

"You worry too much. Just enjoy the ride, like your partner." Henry chuckled.

Alana turned to see Tina lip-locked with a handsome young fan. The youth was a river fae with pale green skin and curly hair—drinking age, but not much more. When the pair finally parted, he staggered back with a dramatic hand-to-heart gesture.

Tina caught Alana's gaze and gave a shrug. "What can I say? He started it. I just obliged."

Then the first bell sounded, and they took their places. Both teams were armed up to—and including—the proverbial teeth. The fights allowed for weapons of all kinds, but not offensive magic. So, the combatants could sprout horns or breath fire, but not put their enemy into a snooze, shrink them to a convenient squishing size, or make them stand still while they poked them with a spear. This was a blood sport, and the audience wanted real action.

Filled with misgivings, Alana slid a dagger from her boot sheath, the whisper of metal against leather like a familiar benediction. Across the circle, one of the Slash drew a kukri knife. The other simply flexed his claws.

By that time, Tina was already weaving on her feet. When the second bell sounded, the fighters advanced, but she stumbled. The gasp of the crowd echoed in the rafters of the makeshift arena. Alana caught a whiff of something sweetly acidic, like strawberries—the poison working in Tina's blood.

The fight spiraled into hell from there. By the time it was over, Henry's rugged face, as seamed as old granite, had been running with tears. Alana saw it from where she was strapped to a gurney, crippled and shorn of everything she'd trained for. And yet, that wasn't the worst of it. Tina was dead, her throat sliced open by the kukri knife. The other casualty was the young river fae who had poisoned her with his kiss. Someone had tricked him into his own death as well as murder.

"Greed never makes for a fair fight," Henry had growled, the only coherent words amid a string of violent curses.

It had been a throwaway line at the time, but one that came back to Alana later. People had placed bets against them, of course, one much bigger than the rest. That wasn't unusual in itself—there was always someone trying to beat the odds. What was remarkable was that it had worked. The Martigen family were the bookmakers. They knew who'd placed that one big bet, and Alana needed that piece of information. It was the only solid lead on whoever had fixed the fight.

The door chimed, and Alana automatically slid off her perch atop the cash desk. Her soles barely hit the floor before she saw the newcomer was Barleycorn. He must have read her surprise, because he laughed.

"I do venture outside my office from time to time, Ms. Beech." Then he gave her a considering appraisal. "You're looking much better than when I saw you last. The store must agree with you."

"Sure. I'm very grateful for the opportunity," she said automatically. "Mr. Corby isn't here."

"I came here to see you."

"Oh?"

Barleycorn moved to stand beside her. "I wanted to see how you were getting on." His eyes were a dark blue rimmed with gold that seemed to give them their own light. Definitely fae eyes, but different from any others she'd seen. Barleycorn was one of a kind.

One Ronan didn't like much, from what she could tell. That put this conversation in an interesting light.

"I'm getting along just fine," she said. "Learning a lot about the business."

No point in telling him she was on the verge of quitting.

"The collectible business as well as the books?" The question was asked lightly, but it made her squirm inside.

"Much of what Mr. Corby buys seems to be garbage."

Barleycorn's smile was bland. "No doubt."

Alana lifted her brows. "Do you have an interest in vintage telephones and eight-track tapes?"

He folded his arms, the emeralds in his cufflinks flashing. He seemed so out of his element in the bookstore, yet Alana knew that wasn't the case. Barleycorn was rooted more deeply in the fae world than even Corby. "Not all commerce is equally good for the community. Not everything should be for sale."

So Barleycorn knew Corby was selling magical knickknacks out the back door. She wasn't sure if that was good or bad for her plans. "And why discuss that with me?"

"I hoped you would be willing to share your observations."

"You want me to spy on my boss?"

"I gave you this job for a reason." His tone was casual, as if he expected her to fall into line.

That annoyed her. "It hardly makes me employee of the month. If you'd asked ahead of time, I would have declined."

The blue-gold eyes turned cold. "You weren't in a position to decline. Nothing about that has changed."

Any inclination she'd had to tell Barleycorn about Tyrell Martigen—or any other part of her plan—died right then. "Are you looking for something in particular?"

His expression remained steady. "A number of parties are currently seeking a dangerous item. It is imperative this item is neutralized before it has the opportunity to work its evil."

"A weapon?" she asked, intrigued despite herself.

"Yes, though it masquerades as more of a faery godmother."

"I wouldn't know," Alana retorted. "My godmother gave up on me when I showed no signs of magical talent."

"Think lucky charm, then," Barleycorn said wryly. "One that helps you realize your secret dreams."

The lamp. He had to mean the lamp. "And when you say neutralize…"

Barleycorn straightened, unfolding his arms and smoothing out his sleeves. "There are only so many meanings for that."

"Why is it so bad if it realizes dreams?"

"How many dreams unexpectedly turn into nightmares?"

Alana's mouth went dry, just like it had before that fatal fight. "I'll be sure to let you know if something turns up."

His smile was empty. "You do that, Ms. Beech."

She stared after Barleycorn long after he left the store. What would he say if he knew she was mistress of the lamp? Would he neutralize her, too?

❧ 7 ❧

Dusk—and Ronan—found Alana in the same place he'd first met her. She sat by her friend's grave, her arms wrapped around her knees. Every line of her body curved inward, that relentlessly straight spine of hers finally bowed. It was a private moment, one where she'd felt safe to drop her guard, and Ronan hesitated to break it.

At the same time, she needed to know there was no such thing as a safe, private place. Not with the enemies she was planning to take on. He cleared his throat.

She raised her head, gray eyes luminous in the soft light. Her open expression showed him the grief she carried, and for an instant, his heart twisted in sympathy. His breath caught before he resolutely shook off the emotion. Doing her a good turn in exchange for a meal was risky enough. Real emotional involvement with his owners would break him. In the end, he'd be forced to betray each one. That was the way of genies.

"How did you find me?" she asked.

"I've told you before. You own me," he replied, sitting by her side. "That cuts both ways."

She gave him a wan smile. "Apparently."

"What are you doing here?" he asked.

"Considering my options."

"You chose a grim place for it." He surveyed the headstones. "It is such a human thing, to be sown in the ground like seeds."

"My mother was forest fae. We bury our dead, too." She plucked a blade of grass.

"And your father's folk?"

"I don't know who he was." She rolled the grass into a tiny ball and cast it aside. "What about yours?"

Ronan ducked his head, remembering wind against his flanks, the hum of air past his wings. "We choose fire and wind at the end. The flames free our souls to become one with the sky."

"You're air fae?" she asked, clearly impressed. "I don't meet your kind that often. Not many of your exiles live in the city."

That didn't surprise him. The air here stank. "You know the history of the conquest?"

"Of course. I learned it in school."

He didn't need a reflection to know the bitterness of his smile. "In school." As if the horror of the Shades' desecration could be reduced to a lecture.

"Did you see it?" Alana asked. "The exile, I mean."

"I did. I saw the Shades."

"Only the dragons stayed behind to fight them," she said slowly. "That's what Barleycorn said. I don't understand why. It was as good as suicide."

Resolutely, he met her serious gray gaze. "They stayed so someday our people can go home."

"Do you think they're still there?"

What a question! No one had ever asked him that. Perhaps he should have been grateful for her curiosity, but she'd used it like a sword blade. And it was clear she'd never met a dragon, or she would know at once he was one of them. Even in their two-legged form, the tall, dark-haired people of Bright Wing were distinctive —and now no more than a footnote in a school lecture. Yes, oh yes, he'd been a prince of the air, powerful and free to hunt and fight. *Had been.*

"I have to believe they're still there." He shrugged, burying his rage as best he could. Someday he would see his family and home again. Someday.

"How did you come to the human realm?" she asked.

"I passed into exile in my owner's luggage." That was how he'd slipped Harin's net. It was his single scrap of luck. He might still be cursed by Harin Blacktongue and forced to offer wishes, but at least he was no longer at his beck and call.

She hugged her knees tighter. "Barleycorn wants to neutralize you."

Ronan leaned back on his elbows, holding onto his anger hard. "I've caught glimpses of John Barleycorn since coming to the human realm. Exile seems to have wiped away his sense of humor. He used to be something of a—how do you say it?—party animal."

She let lose a strangled laugh. "That's hard to picture."

"We were all different back then." Why was he telling her this? It had nothing to do with solving their problems. It had nothing to do with anything—yet he couldn't stop talking. The same thing had happened last night. He'd missed the back and forth of casual conversation.

This was Alana's doing, offering her friendship until he couldn't help but take it. She was so strong, but so naive. That frank openness made her vulnerable. He could read her far too easily, and he could already guess what that first wish would be. Even so, she was a drug he couldn't resist. The beast inside him— torn, bloodied stump that it was—responded to her kindness like a feral thing shyly snatching scraps from her fingers. She made him remember who he was. What he might have been.

The truth was, he wanted to possess her in ways that simply couldn't happen, because it would destroy them both. He palmed his face, grinding the weariness from his eyes. What was he going to do about her? Once she was gone, the withdrawal would be hell.

"What does Barleycorn have against you?" Alana asked.

"He knows the truth about me. I told you I was a weapon."

"Yes."

"What do you think happens to a person when I grant their wish?"

"They're happy?"

"For a day, a year, twenty years. The length of time depends on the wisdom of the person doing the wish. The smarter the wish, the longer it seems to last."

"But?"

"Sooner or later, they want another. No one is perfectly happy every day of their lives."

"So they make another wish."

"Of course they do. They always want something more."

"And eventually, they run out of wishes."

He nodded. "And then they're sad."

That was the understatement of all time. However long his owners lasted between wishes one and two, barely any time elapsed between two and three. The second wish never worked as planned. And then the heartbreak began.

"So Barleycorn is basing his assessment on a string of customer complaints?"

"Essentially."

"That hardly seems fair."

Ronan wanted to say it was absolutely fair, but all he could do was shake his head. The spell that made him a nightmare wouldn't permit more than that. Otherwise, who would ever make a single wish?

His first owner had wished for a beautiful girl child—as harmless a request as could be. Wish two was for a brilliant match for the darling daughter when she turned seventeen. Wish three was to save her when she struggled to give them a grandchild. Then they'd needed a fourth wish to save the grandchild, but there'd been no fourth wish. Their darling girl faded away in grief, mourning her child until she joined it in the ground beneath a willow tree.

His second wish-maker had been a soldier who wanted glory, and Ronan gave it to him. But then the brave captain had to repeat that success to maintain his good name, so his second wish requested another chance for fame and fortune. When that plan went awry, his third wish had been to save his men from disaster. There'd been no fourth wish to save the captain's limbs from the surgeon's knife, of course. He'd died a beggar.

But they had been fortunate, compared to others. The wishes were a trap. The only ones to escape were those who had something Harin wanted—fortune, power, or extraordinary magic. He'd grant a fourth wish if they had an acceptable trade. The fourth wish didn't guarantee happiness, either, but Harin would make bargain after bargain until they had nothing left to give. Two wishes seemed enough to make addicts of the wisest man or woman, however powerful they were.

Ronan's only comfort was that Harin Blacktongue wasn't around in this realm to make those final deals, so the damage stopped at three and the lamp moved on. His past owners never recovered. It was as if all their life's luck had run out, but at least they died as themselves. Those Harin had touched eventually became his willing servants, corrupted to their core. Ronan always wondered what piece of their hearts they had, in their final desperation, bargained away.

Alana chose that moment to reach out and take his hand—again. Her skin was cool from the chill of the graveyard air. "I'm sorry this happened to you."

Pain shuddered through his chest, and he took a deep breath to fight it down. "You're kind, but I've had time to get used to it."

"Still, I think I'm going to take your advice and go to work for Martigen."

"Ah..." Ronan sat up, folding his free hand around their joined ones. "That's what I came here to talk to you about. I spent the afternoon following young Tyrell over hill and dale."

"And?" Alana inched closer.

They must have made an interesting picture, heads bowed together like conspiratorial lovers. Romantic, except for the graveyard location and the fact he could never, ever have this woman as he wanted. Oh, he could pleasure one, sure enough, but not as a mate. Not as anything more than a physical act, because sooner or later...

"I followed him from house to business to club," he said. "Martigen met with important families of the fae. I knew the names, if not all the members of this generation."

"What did they talk about?"

"I don't know. I couldn't get close enough."

She squinted at him doubtfully.

Ronan felt suddenly inadequate. "I wasn't designed to be a spy. I can't read lips or eavesdrop from a mile away. You want a leprechaun for that."

"Okay, fine," Alana said, patting the air to calm him down. "What do you *think* it was about?"

"He visited noble families, regardless of their tribe. Fire fae, water fae, earth fae," Ronan mused. "What do all the groups have in common, regardless of business alliances or family connections?"

"The fights," Alana said without hesitation. "Even if they despise each other, they'll all attend. It's neutral ground, and they all need to let off steam."

Ronan understood. In the human world, they had to obey human laws, but fae were still half-wild. Blood sports satisfied a thirst no human spectacle could quench.

"If it's about the fights, I have a chance of uncovering something," she continued. "I understand how that world works. I just have to get close to Tyrell, because he runs the bookmaking part of the family business."

Her mouth was set in a determined line that made Ronan want to press his lips to hers. He could almost taste her brave spirit from where he sat an arm's-length away. But it would be oh so much sweeter with their bodies pressed skin to skin. Her eyes seemed to shimmer in the softening light, making a portal Ronan wished he could enter. Inside this woman was a world he longed to visit—but he knew better. He pulled his hand from hers, forcing himself to remain apart. His hand felt lost without hers, as if she were the only thing binding him to the earth.

It was time he shut this—whatever it was—between them down. "How do you plan to approach Martigen for a job?" he asked.

Alana heaved a sigh of frustration. "That's why I came here to think. I don't have a lot of choices, especially if I cross Barleycorn. He wants me at Corby's in case a certain lamp turns up."

Suddenly things were making a pattern he didn't like. "Barleycorn will be watching you."

"All the more reason not to be working in the exact place where that lamp is supposed to turn up."

"True."

"My main option is to show up at Martigen Industries and ask for a job, but Barleycorn and Corby will be lousy references."

"And your other options?"

Alana sighed. "There aren't any other good choices."

There was one, but he hated it. All the same, the suggestion welled inside him, driven by Harin's spell. They were words he'd said a thousand fateful times. "You could use a wish. You've got two others to spare."

Alana laughed ruefully, casting a long look at her dead partner's headstone. The inscription was unreadable in the gloom, but the white marble glowed in the final, fading shreds of daylight.

"Maybe. I wouldn't be able to be a guard at all unless you'd healed me. You've already got me halfway there."

Ronan cursed himself. That was exactly why he'd helped her before, so she'd associate his powers with something good. It was a useful sales trick, but now he wished he'd left her alone. Better crippled than cursed.

"You have to say it out loud." His voice sounded like claws on gravel.

He couldn't bear to raise his head and meet her gaze, just in case that made her trust him more. Ronan held his breath, hyper-aware of every nuance of her being—every shift in posture, every strand of her fair hair lifting in the breeze. Alana was at a tipping point. She could go on as she was, or she could start walking the path of Ronan's curse.

A long silence followed, so long he almost believed she'd avoided the snare. But then she spoke.

"I wish I would get a job tomorrow as Tyrell Martigen's personal bodyguard."

❧ 8 ❧

A week later, Alana intercepted a female with a clipboard by stepping into her path.

The woman's surprise quickly darkened to annoyance. "Excuse me?"

"Identification, please," Alana said, keeping her voice polite. She'd memorized the pictures of all the Martigen staff, and this person wasn't in the file. *Late forties, human, professional dress but she's recently stopped wearing her wedding band.*

The woman bridled, but Alana didn't care. The only way to Tyrell Martigen and his entourage was through her, and bodyguards weren't paid to be people-pleasers.

"It's all right, Alana," Tyrell said. "Sheila's here from the Waterfront Foundation."

He referred to the charity group raising money for a new children's hospital. Alana stepped aside, earning a scathing glance from Sheila. They were opposites, Alana with fair hair and a dark pantsuit, and Sheila with salon-corrected dark hair and an ensemble in winter white. The woman all but vanished against the pale marble lining the lobby.

Alana memorized Sheila's face just as she had all the others, pinning it on her mental suspect board. Until she'd figured out who was involved with the Corby-Barleycorn-Martigen fight-fixing, murder, and lamp-theft plot—not to mention figuring out what exactly that plot entailed—no one escaped consideration.

Sheila handed Tyrell an envelope. "The mayor requested I deliver this personally, so you can include the names of the major donors in your remarks. They are, of course, to be kept confidential until the gala."

"Consider me a vault." Tyrell signed for the envelope, then gave the woman a charming smile. She colored slightly as she retrieved her pen and hurried off.

In the time Alana had been working for Martigen, she'd noted his skill handling the swarms of people seeking his attention. The fact he remembered all their names—and remained unfailingly polite—was a feat in itself.

As soon as Sheila left, the entourage resumed walking and Tyrell's assistant started yammering. "The car will pick you up at seven to reach the art gallery at seven-thirty. Meet and greet, cocktails, speeches at eight-thirty, your presentation to the donors at nine, then dinner and dancing after that."

"I'll be gone by nine-thirty, off to the soiree at the Unseelie Club. Have the car ready."

The assistant nodded, making notes. Meanwhile, the assistant's assistant pushed forward. "Mr. Martigen, sir, I have Henry Blackwell on the line for you."

Alana's ears perked up at the mention of her coach's name. "Tell him I'll call him back," Tyrell replied. Then he turned to Alana. "Maybe I should send you to find out what the old bear wants."

"I'm happy to do whatever is required," she replied with a bow of her head.

"Of course you are," he said cheerfully. "You're settling in very well. I'd hardly know you were ever injured in the circle."

Alana kept her expression bland. "I'm fit for duty."

He laughed. "Otherwise, you'd still be at the bookstore instead of here. But seriously, I'm glad things are working out. Anything you need, just ask."

Oddly, she thought he meant it. Tyrell Martigen wanted to be liked. When they reached the entrance of the huge office building, he greeted the doorman by name and asked after his daughter's graduation plans.

They'd barely made it to the courtyard when the mood of the entourage turned quiet. A knot of five men descended on them, Tyrell's father in the lead. She'd seen father and son meet before, and it was always strained but carefully polite.

With a twinge of surprise, she saw one of the newcomers was Randall, the demi-fae who'd tried to bully her in Barleycorn's office. So he'd gotten the job he'd interviewed for. That said a lot about his new boss.

Unlike his son, Hugo Martigen was square, dark, and as lovable as a rabid wolverine. All Tyrell's hangers-on scattered like sparrows, leaving only Alana and her fellow guard on either side of their employer.

Instinctively, she touched the knife sheath beneath her jacket, where multiple blades were strapped for easy access. All the guards carried them, but only for use if things got nasty. Knives were quiet, discreet, and easy to enchant if something happened that humans shouldn't see. Fae rarely used firearms except for sport—they had plenty of better options when it came to serious long-range violence. Plus, many refused to touch cold iron if they could help it.

"Father," Tyrell said evenly. "Is there something I can do for you?"

Hugo waved a hand, and his men stepped away, giving him privacy. The older man glared at Alana, expecting her to do the same, but she eyed Tyrell pointedly until he gave her the nod. She backed away, but not so far that she couldn't catch at least some of the conversation.

"Did you call the meeting?" Hugo asked his son.

"Yes. I called on each member personally," Tyrell replied.

Members of what? Alana wondered. Ronan had seen Tyrell going from door to door after the scene at Comfy Chair Books and Collectibles. Was that what he'd been doing?

"Do we have news to tell them?" Hugo demanded.

"Not yet."

From the corner of her eye, Alana saw Hugo draw himself up until he loomed over his son. Tyrell paled, but didn't move. When Hugo spoke, she barely caught the words. "There will be consequences if we don't deliver."

"I know."

"I don't think you *do* know, or you would be weeping with fear. The investor wants his pound of flesh, and if the cabal can't meet his demands, he'll take his due in gold instead."

"We don't have the cash flow for that. We'd be dead in the water."

"Ah, so you *are* paying attention." Hugo leaned in so he was nose to nose with Tyrell. "Then maybe you'll do the one thing I asked and take care of business."

"I can only do what's possible," Tyrell replied stiffly.

"If it were easy, I would have done it myself."

"Then maybe you should, Dad."

Hugo snorted his disgust and wheeled away from Tyrell, shouldering past him toward the entrance of the office building. His henchmen followed with clockwork efficiency. As he passed, Randall cast Alana a sour look.

Alana and the other guard, Bruce, came up to Tyrell. "Where to, boss?" Bruce asked, as if nothing had happened.

Tyrell gave a soft laugh. "I love you guys. Let's go to my rooms. It's getting late, and I need to dress for tonight."

They started toward the building across the way. Martigen Towers sat on the southern edge of the downtown, and it was made up of three skyscrapers arranged around a park-like courtyard. The place they'd just left was the business headquarters. The other two towers were residential, with the top floors reserved for the Martigen family, friends, and key employees. Alana wondered if bodyguards ever get one of the fancy apartments.

They made it most of the way across the courtyard, past the busier pathways and into the sheltered corner leading to the first of the residential buildings. Alana began to daydream about grabbing dinner and telling Ronan about her day, but not so much that her guard was completely down.

That was lucky, because the attack came too fast to see. Figures sprang from the evening shadows, cutting off their retreat and any hope of advancing toward the door. Alana got an impression of short, dark figures no taller than a child, but they were squat and strong. Kobolds? But those fae were miners, and didn't move like dark lightning. These creatures were new to her, and they weren't friendly.

She punched the alarm on her wristband, summoning backup. From the corner of her eye, she saw Bruce do the same. Tyrell, however, stood wide-eyed and frozen. That was the difference training made.

The attacker in front of her flicked his hand, and a blade spun through the air. Alana pushed Tyrell to the ground, using her body as cover. The knife bounced as it hit the pavement, and she had a glimpse of a carved antler handle. There was no time to grab for it. The one who'd thrown the weapon was closing in.

Now she could see a broad-featured face with a lot of black beard and a predator's eyeteeth. He was holding a second knife, this one with a wicked curved blade. She kicked, aiming for Short and Hairy's head, but he slashed, the knife slicing through pant leg and deep into her shin. Alana yelped, but followed through with a solid hook to the jaw. He staggered, and her next blow sent him sprawling.

Bruce had a second opponent down, but victory was short-lived. Just as Alana helped Tyrell to his feet, the shadows spewed a flock of squeaking, flapping horrors. Within seconds, they were swarmed. Alana swiped at the air around her head as tiny claws tugged at her hair. The creatures reminded her of bats, but they seemed to have no heads. They were just scraps of darkness with teeth and talons.

Bruce collapsed under the hungry cloud. Alana took a step toward him, flinching as she put weight on her bleeding leg, but Tyrell's shout made her turn his way. One of the creatures had fastened itself to his neck. His eyes were wide with terror as he clutched at the thing, unable to tear it away as it gorged on the blood leaking from his throat.

Frantically drawing her own knife, she slashed at the flying things as they swooped into her face. They aimed for the eyes and throat, disorienting their prey. She grabbed Tyrell's jacket and dragged him closer, then drove the knife point into the body of the thing sucking his blood. It shrieked, a wail that sent every one of its kin fluttering higher into the air. Then it dropped to the ground with a juicy splat.

Now that it was still, Alana got a good look. It was shaped like a starfish, with claws along the limbs and a round mouth in the middle of its belly. Blood oozed from it, but not all of it was red. Most was pure black.

"Alana," Tyrell barked.

She spun, barely avoiding the knife blade of her first attacker. She threw her own weapon in one smooth flick. Short and Hairy went down, the knife buried in one eye. This time, he wouldn't get up.

Bruce was scrambling to his hands and knees, bites covering his face and hands. Alana grabbed him by the shoulders, pulling him up.

"Get inside," Tyrell ordered, holding open the door.

Alana lunged for safety, shoving Bruce and Tyrell into the lobby. She'd barely closed and locked the door before the swarm was back, plastering themselves to the plate glass. There seemed to be more than before—enough to block out the first red banners of the sunset.

She stared at the overlapping web of clawed limbs. They seemed to be pulsing with the need to dig through the glass and into her body. "What the hell is this about?"

Pale as milk, Bruce grabbed one of the pillars that supported the vaulted ceiling. With his other hand, he fished out his phone. "Reinforcements are already on their way. I'm telling them to bring flamethrowers."

Alana could hear the sirens. "You need medical help."

"I'll tell them that, too. Get the boss upstairs."

Although Bruce was right—their charge was their first concern—she hated to leave the other bodyguard alone. "Are you sure?"

"Hell, yeah. I'm going to enjoy the show."

More concerned with escape, Tyrell had already pushed the call button for the elevator. He was braced against the wall, one hand to the wound in his neck. Alana limped his way, then helped him into the elevator once the door opened. They both leaned against the mirrored wall of the car, breathing hard.

"Bruce will be all right," Tyrell said. "I've seen him survive worse."

Still slumped against the wall, she rolled her head to meet his eyes. "How often does this happen?"

"Not very. I'm the quiet one in the family."

"Good to hear," she said. Her leg throbbed.

Tyrell leaned forward, gently kissing her on the cheek. "Thank you for saving my life."

As kisses went, it was innocent enough, but a shiver ran through her just the same. She should have been attracted to Tyrell. He was smart, handsome, and power clung to him like aftershave—yet he just didn't check her boxes. Maybe she didn't go for the rich tycoon type.

Or maybe it was the fact she was really there to unveil his

secrets and—oh, look—she was about to gain access to his private rooms.

The elevator stopped and a panel slid back, revealing a keypad. Rather than press his thumb to the reader right away, he angled his body so she was caught between his hard chest and the wall. He leaned down, his face just inches from hers.

"What do you think, Alana? We have a connection now, a shared experience of danger. Liaisons have been founded on less."

Another shiver coursed through her, but it wasn't the good kind. "I think adrenaline clouds the mind, sir."

"Always the professional, my Alana."

The doors slid open to reveal the vestibule of his penthouse apartment. She caught a glimpse of dark wallpaper, darker paintings, and an expensive mirror. "Come inside," he said, taking her hand.

"I'm supposed to deliver you to safety, that's all," she said. "There's a crisis downstairs."

He pulled her after him. "You're hurt."

"My wound stopped bleeding."

"I doubt it." He tugged her hand.

She stumbled forward, finding him surprisingly strong. The elevator doors slid closed behind her as Tyrell steered her to the window. Far, far below, emergency lights flashed red and blue. Slipping a hand around her waist, he pulled her close, clearly meaning to pick up where that almost-kiss had ended.

"You see, there's the cavalry," he said. "There's nothing to worry about."

"Oh?"

"They're fae. We keep them on speed dial for things the regular police won't understand."

She pulled away. "Like the dead bodies?"

Clearly disgruntled, he stepped back from the window, touching the wound in his neck. His fingers came away scarlet. "The men use an onsite incinerator. My father had it installed."

Her face went numb with shock. It wasn't the idea itself, but the casual way he'd said it. Of course they had staff who disposed of bodies—it was part of doing business at the Martigen family firm.

"What's going on, Tyrell?" It felt odd to use his first name, but he had crossed the line between the professional and personal already. "I can't help you unless I understand what you're up against."

"What *I'm* up against? It started out as my father's idea, and now he's dragging me down, too." He heaved an angry sigh. "And getting my employees hurt. You're bleeding."

She looked down at her leg. Sure enough, blood glistened on the black fabric of her slacks. "I've had worse."

His mouth flattened into a hard line. "Watch where you sit with that. Let me get you a cloth." With that, he left the room.

Alana examined her surroundings. The decor was textbook alpha male, as if the designer was trying to convey billionaire pheromones in chrome and black leather. Curious, she surveyed the walls and shelves, searching for clues. There was no sign of the betting records she wanted. Those might be on computer, but she bet Tyrell, like Barleycorn's goblin, kept his fae-related business dealings in a traditional leather-bound book. Unfortunately, there were very few books and even less art on display.

The exception was the oval mirror in the vestibule, which had to be an antique. The wooden frame was ornately carved and coated in gold leaf. The glass itself was oddly dark, as if it had lost the silver that made it a mirror. When she got close, her face was only a ghost.

Except...behind her wide-eyed image, with the hair straggling from her ponytail, was a forest. At first, she thought it was a painting beneath the glass, but the trees moved in a silent breeze. Repeating the same move she'd made when peering into Corby's office, she leaned to the left, changing the angle of her sight. Mountains filled the horizon. When she leaned right, ignoring the stabbing agony in her leg, she saw the ragged roofline of what might have been a castle. Foreboding spiraled through her.

Somewhere in the apartment, water began to run, reminding Alana she wasn't alone. She retreated from the mirror, oddly reluctant to turn her back to it. Where was that forest? What was she looking at? A familiar crawling sensation reminded her where she'd seen a smaller mirror just like it—Corby's office. The two men had been arguing about the lamp, and they both had mirrors. There had to be a connection.

What was going on?

She'd wished herself into this job to find that out. It might have been easier just to wish for answers instead. It would be safer. They'd all nearly been killed moments ago. She could prevent disaster just by asking directly for what she needed. Alana held that thought a moment, testing it with her mind. It was tempting, but no. She'd find better answers if she put some effort into finding the right questions first.

The argument with herself might have gone on, but that creeping, watching sensation chased her back to the main room. Ignoring Tyrell's concerns about getting blood on the furniture, she sat by a low coffee table littered with paper. Beside her was Tyrell's discarded jacket, smeared with blood.

The envelope Sheila had given him protruded from the pocket. Before she could talk herself out of it, she slid the packet out and checked its thickness with her fingers. As she'd suspected, it was too fat for just a piece of paper with donors' names—so what was Sheila delivering on behalf of the mayor? The flap was glued shut, of course, but what was to say that it hadn't been torn in the scuffle downstairs?

Alana pried the corner open, revealing a thick stack of currency. She couldn't make out the value of the bills, but it didn't matter. The point was the mayor was sending cash to Tyrell. Why?

She stuffed the envelope back before he caught her snooping.

First the attack, then the weird mirror, and now this. Alarm was building inside her like steam in a kettle. Sooner or later, she was going to have to let it out or else explode. She squirmed, wondering where Tyrell had gone.

Her gaze fell on the mess on the table, a combination of magazines and official-looking reports on the investment potential of this business or that. Scattered among them were crumpled papers she knew all too well. Betting slips for the underground fights. The Martigen family served as the bookmakers—and she wanted to know who had won big the night Tina died.

She picked up one of the crumpled slips, turning it over. These always had a name and an amount. She read the information before letting it fall back to the table. Then she scanned others. There were different names, but no doubt those wagers—and the people who made them—had been in Tyrell's pocket.

Maybe that was why the mayor was sending bundles of cash. Humans sometimes bet on fae fights, if they happened to know the right people.

Gambling. Cash flow. The investor. The connection was almost within her grasp. She *had* to find his betting books.

But that would have to wait. Tyrell was back, washed, combed, and in a clean shirt. His neck was neatly bandaged. No wonder he'd taken a while. "I'll take you to the bathroom if you'd like to clean your wound."

She studied him, taking in his finely drawn features. "Was that attack just now a warning?"

A fine line appeared between his brows. She'd taken him off guard, but not as much as she would have liked. He made an impatient gesture. "The family business is very complicated."

"Tell me," she insisted. "You're in danger, and it's my business to protect you."

He shrugged. "Let's just say it was an incentive to meet performance goals."

"Your dad said something about cash-flow problems."

"All businesses have liquidity issues from time to time."

Her gaze strayed around the room, taking in the home entertainment unit, the betting slips, and the antique mirror shimmering through the doorway—an entryway to who knew where. Some of that cash flowed right here to create this deluxe lifestyle—but not all.

She gave him a stern look. "The fights are what's keeping you afloat, aren't they? If you need quick cash, just have a word with the right people and the match goes your way."

"Alana the Incorruptible. That's how you got that name, right? You'd never play the game." His mouth curled up in one corner.

Shame burned in her gut. She'd meant to confront him—to force the truth into the open. All she'd managed to do was amuse him. "Who got rich the night my partner died?"

"Leave it alone," he said, almost gently. "You won't find answers here. The fae don't play fair in or out of the fighting circle."

She might have found a snappy comeback, except her wits had turned to dust.

There was a face in the mirror, and it was watching them.

❧   9   ❧

"Describe the face," Ronan said later.

Alana had been slow to arrive home that night. He'd known through their bond that something was up, and he'd been on the verge of going in search of her. Then she'd dragged herself through the door, bloody and exhausted.

"The image wasn't entirely clear," she said. "Everything in the mirror was dark."

She was sitting at the table, if that boneless sprawl of fatigue counted as sitting. Ronan put a cup of tea in front of her before bending to see to her leg. The fact Martigen had neglected her injuries said far more than all the young tycoon's smiles and handshakes.

"You don't need to do that," Alana said as Ronan cut away her already-ruined pant leg.

"No, I don't," he agreed, holding his palm over the wound and summoning the golden light that held a genie's healing power, "but I'm not a grinning worm in a bespoke business suit, either. I know enough to be grateful for your courage. Describe the face."

"It was male, I think, with long, bony features and pale green skin. I couldn't see the hair, as if he were wearing a hood."

Ronan focused on her face, attention dragged from his work. "And the eyes?"

She shuddered. "Bright. Big. He didn't seem to have eyelids."

"The color?"

"It was odd. They were horrible, staring and evil, but the color was beautiful. Purple. Violet." She picked up the tea in both hands and drank. "I don't know what to call it."

Ronan blocked his welling emotions, forcing himself to finish sealing the knife wound on Alana's slim, strong leg. He moved the healing light in deliberate strokes, soothing and cleansing. The cut wasn't deep, but it was long and he didn't stop until it had closed to a thin white line.

Keeping her safe and well was important, but so was having something to focus on besides Alana's report. Once, such news would have made him explode into a frenzy of fire and fang. He'd learned the hard way his temper was worse than useless against the Shades.

Because that was what Alana had glimpsed—the nightmare that had trampled his world. Pain ripped through him, emotion so raw it was physical. He took a deep breath, choking it back. Self-control was what he needed now—the few times anyone had beaten the Shades, it had been with granite nerves and steel-bright wits.

The healing was done, and the golden light absorbed back into his palm. Slowly, he rose to his feet. "The creatures that attacked you were foot soldiers of the Shades. The water fae you saw in the mirror was named Harin."

"Water fae?" Alana's eyes were huge. "He didn't look like any fae I've ever seen."

"He changed as he grew corrupted. We call him Blacktongue now for his betrayal of our realm. He surrendered his waters so the Shades could enter our realm."

Alana set down her tea, her exhausted slouch gone. "The thing in the mirror is working with the Shades?"

"He is one of them now." His voice had gone rough, old hatred closing his throat. "Blacktongue believed he could buy his survival, and the Shades took everything he gave."

Alana stood to face him. "I don't understand. I mean, sure, some mirrors are sentient, but why did I see someone from a different place that..." She paused. "The Shades are somehow communicating between realms, aren't they?"

He could feel the warmth of her body and wanted to reach out, but he couldn't tell who he meant to comfort—Alana or himself. "It is pure Shade magic. They call it the Shimmer, two reflections that coincide between realms."

"Figures." She folded her arms, which showed off her slender body. "I've never heard anything good about magic mirrors."

"They're growing stronger if they were able to send a handful of servants into this world. That is how it happened with us— scouting parties came before the final invasion."

"Invasion?"

"Harin was at the center of things then, too."

"How?"

"I knew him in his youth," Ronan said. Darkness had gathered imperceptibly back then—a bit here or there, but never enough to call foul until it was too late. "He was a scholar, curious about everything. No doubt he stumbled on some means of contact with the Shades, not knowing what he'd found."

"And then?"

"Then they wooed him to their side. Or threatened. It barely matters now. All it takes is one fool to unlock the door, and in they come. Now he sits at the right hand of Ebor the Golden, and he leads the Shade King's armies to war."

He remembered that moment when he saw the Shimmer on the black lake that had been Harin's last home. To build a mirror of that size would have taken a century—yet all that time, the water fae had smiled and sat at Ronan's table, drinking Ronan's wine.

"What do the Shades want?" Alana asked.

Anger pounded, a war drum sounding throughout his body. "Whatever they can get. A world to conquer. Provisions for their armies. Palaces for their lords." He gave a harsh laugh. "Whatever amusements help pass an eternity soaked in violence."

Alana went paler than before, but she didn't flinch. "And they were the ones who put you in the lamp?"

"Yes." He held her gaze, falling into her clear gray eyes. "I'm still their prisoner. If they take me back, get possession of my lamp, you can never trust me. Promise me you'll remember that."

She couldn't trust him now, but under the power of a creature like Blacktongue, he would be a far worse monster.

"I'm not a fool," she said quietly. Then she took his face between her palms. He moved to pull away, but she gave a quick shake of her head, demanding he stay still. "Listen to me. I will fight to keep those things out of my world."

"As you should."

"I'll be fighting for you, too. I'll help you if I can."

Her words sank into his soul, cool and sweet as a healing balm. Also insanely optimistic, but that barely mattered right then. She'd made him feel a little less alone. Before he knew what he was doing, Ronan bent his head, his lips hovering over hers. Her breath was sweet with the honey from her tea.

A last grain of sanity held him back for one heartbeat, then two. But then he surrendered, his need to touch her too powerful to cage any longer. Her lips melted under his, as smooth and soft as he'd imagined. Her hands slid from his face and roved through his hair, caressing and demanding in ways he'd forgotten. He had been solitary for so long.

And he shouldn't touch Alana now. It would lead to heart-break, but he was like a drowning man coming up for air. He couldn't *not* breathe.

He tasted her again and again, suckling her ripe lips until they were flushed with kisses. Her skin was soft and pale against his, like starlight against tawny desert sands. Ronan ached to feel the strength of her body work against his. She might not be one of the Bright Wing dragons, but she would give as good as she got, matching strength for strength. Alana would know enough to test his mastery even as she comforted his sorrows.

By the Wheel, she was nothing like the noble females he'd taken to his bed. She worked for her bread, claiming no pedigree or power. Bloody and disheveled, she stood before him now, her clothes beyond repair. Yet, she was everything he wanted.

She'd stripped off her suit jacket, letting it fall to the floor. Her crisp white blouse was stained and wilted, but her weapons shone securely in their sheaths and holsters. He approved—and began helping her out of the buckles and straps. A lusty male had to help his lover shed her defenses, but he'd never done it quite so literally before.

When she finally discarded the rest of her clothes, his gaze feasted on the sleek shape of her limbs. Scars tracked across her body like angular lace, or poetry in a savage script he did not know. The beauty of that desecration surprised him. They were her story, and he was suddenly glad she hadn't let him wipe them away. He buried his face in her shoulder, breathing in her rich scent, committing it to his memory and soul.

He lifted her by the waist, and her long legs wrapped around him. Slender though she was, her breasts were surprisingly full, the peach lace of her bra barely enough to hold them. He tongued one nipple into his mouth and sucked it to a peak, enjoying the rough sensation of the fabric against his lips. He did the same with the other, coaxing a low moan from Alana's throat.

She released the firm clasp of her thighs and grabbed the front of his T-shirt, pulling him hard toward the bed. Ronan let himself be led, let her peel the shirt over his head and press her lips to his throat. Her teeth scraped his skin, a gentle bite of possession that made him growl.

His hands skimmed her arms, feeling lean muscle beneath the

velvet softness of her skin. The combination intrigued him. She wasn't simply a siren or a warrior, but an intoxicating combination of both.

He pushed her down to the bed, parting her knees. She wore a slip of fabric there, barely a token to modesty. He ran his tongue over the softness of her inner thigh, drinking in the warm female scent. It was a soft, unmistakable perfume that had nothing to do with cosmetics. It was pure Alana, as unique as her.

He kissed her, tasting her through the useless undergarment. In a fit of impatience, he ripped through the flimsy thing and tossed it aside. When she drew breath to protest, he took her with his mouth and turned her curse to a helpless moan. She opened wider, inviting him in with that scent, warmth, and wetness. He circled her nub with his thumb, drawing a shudder from her frame. She was primed, sensitive, ready for what he had to give. With his tongue and teeth, he gave it.

When his hands found her breasts again, he finally released them from the cage of lace and wire. Alana was breathing hard, her eyes unfocussed. She threaded her fingers through his hair, pulling him down to find his mouth, then rolling him over to run long-fingered hands over his flesh as she straddled him. He was hard, but she teased him until he ached with agonized need. Heat and cold and incandescent need tore through him, urging him to give in to her demands.

When it was impossible to hold on, he entered her, groaning his appreciation of her tight, wet heat. When he withdrew and thrust again, Alana moved with him, using all her muscles. He pushed once more, matching angle to angle as she rose to return the pleasure tenfold. She was like lightning to his core, shorting every conscious thought. The beast in him broke its cage, driving them both to mindless pleasure.

Later, his head spun, filled with the aftermath of sensation. Impressions of Alana were foremost—the wild woman who had ridden him moments ago, then the softly breathing form now draped in his arms. At the edges of his mind floated broken images of his mountain home—scraps of landscape, glimpses of half-forgotten faces. Alana had stirred emotions that in turn unlocked the past.

Grief and anger unspooled from somewhere deep in his soul, filling him until the pressure made it hard to breathe. He sighed, releasing it slowly to relieve the ache. He'd sworn to protect his home, and he'd failed.

He turned his head to study Alana's sleeping form. He had nothing to offer her—or any woman—until he had broken the lamp's curse. Then he could reclaim his father's realm and lay it at her feet. He took her hands in his, pressing his lips to her battered fingers. "Mistress, I am yours to command."

He spoke the words quietly, so she didn't awake. That was fine, because the hope in them was so new, so fragile, he wasn't ready to share his impossible dream. *What if I was free of the lamp? What if there was a future we could share?*

I am yours to command. A genie said such things a thousand times a day. But this time, his words had a very different meaning. Alana had given him the courage to fight again, to redeem his honor and free his home. Somehow, he would go back and win the battle he'd begun.

Alana was everything to him. She had brought him back to life.

Alana awoke curled in Ronan's arms, her head cushioned against his chest. She quickly closed her eyes, not wanting to admit the night was over, and breathed in the spicy scent of his skin. Her acting wasn't good enough, though. His fingers slid over her bare shoulder to twirl a lock of her hair.

"A person's breathing changes when they wake up." His words echoed in his chest, rumbling beneath her ear.

She pushed into a sitting position to better see him. One

corner of his mouth quirked up in a very male smirk and she automatically reached for the bedsheet, folding it around her.

"Good morning," she said before yawning.

The expression in his eyes softened. "Good morning."

Such a small phrase to capture everything that had passed between them. She was struck by the thick sweep of his dark lashes. How had she never noticed those lashes before? And how did anyone look that good first thing in the morning? She pushed her hair out of her eyes, suddenly self-conscious.

He reached up, cupping the back of her head, then pulled her down for a kiss. It was slow and greedy. Ronan was nothing if not thorough. Already, that act of possession felt familiar. If he was supposed to be her slave, there was absolutely nothing subservient in his lovemaking.

He rolled her over, so her back was pressed into the mattress, then caged her with his arms and legs. "When are you required to show up for your work?" he asked, the hint of a growl just below the surface.

"It's my day off," she replied. It was suddenly hard to concentrate, much less form words. "I would love nothing better than to spend it right here. It's been a long, dry spell these last months."

"Meaning?"

"Not many guys want a woman who can bench press their own weight."

"Fools," Ronan repeated, the gleam in his eye telling her that he was making plans.

Reluctantly, she sat up, forcing him to sit back on his heels. The morning light seeping around the curtains gilded him, showing off every curve and shadow of his honed body. *Yowzah!* Her mouth all but watered, but she clung fiercely to her resolve. "Day off or not, there was a Shade attack. We need to figure out how they got on this side of the mirrors."

Ronan's features hardened as he grew serious. "From your description, those were foot soldiers. Mere minions. In some ways, that is good news. It means the Shades aren't ready to send a full army yet."

"Yes, but it's the thin edge of the wedge."

"I know." With a regretful sigh, he rolled off the bed, finding his jeans. "What do you propose to do?"

"What are you capable of, besides healing and granting wishes?" she asked.

He raised a brow, and Alana flushed. "Okay," she added, "and besides that."

"I can transport small items by magic. Plus, I can provide transportation via carpet, as long as one is supplied. I'm also rather good at finding lost camels."

Alana considered. Those were all handy talents, but not obvious showstoppers. Then again, what would it take to stop an invasion from another realm?

"I don't have a plan," she said. "Not yet, but I figure it's like any fighting hold. It's not about brute strength. It's about finding the weak joint, then putting the pressure there."

"Targeted resistance." Ronan picked up his shirt, letting it dangle from one hand. "Go on."

It was hard to marshal her thoughts with so much bare-chested glory in the room, but she did her best. "Let's recap. For whatever reason, Blacktongue opened a door to the Shades, letting them into your world. The invasion ended with most of the fae fleeing to this world. Now Blacktongue, presumably still on the Shades' payroll, is using magic mirrors to communicate with the exiled fae. I've personally seen one mirror in Corby's office, and another in Tyrell's front hall."

To her great disappointment, Ronan pulled his shirt on. She understood the impulse. Talking about the mirrors made her feel vulnerable, and she pulled the blankets more tightly around her naked body.

"If yesterday's attack is any indication, the Shades use threats to get what they want. Right now, everyone is running scared, including Tyrell and Hugo Martigen. I think they are the Shades' contacts in this community. From the sound of it, Hugo was on board first, but now Tyrell is dragged into it."

"That makes sense," Ronan agreed. "And contact has probably been ongoing for some time."

"But something's changed. The fae here keep their existence more or less secret from the humans, and the Shades must know that. And yet, yesterday they mounted a daylight attack on Tyrell because he's not delivering the goods fast enough."

"Risky," he agreed.

"Maybe the Shades don't care about secrecy anymore, because they'll soon invade this world, too." Alana jammed her fingers into her tangled hair, as if that would stimulate her thoughts.

"So where in all this spiderweb of circumstance are you going to find your pressure point?" he asked, taking a seat beside her and wrapping an arm around her waist.

"I've got one more person to talk to. My old coach, Henry."

"What would he know?"

"I still haven't given up on the gambling angle, or that someone rigged my last fight." Or that someone had poisoned Tina—an otherwise unbeatable fighter—to win big against the odds. "The perpetrator has to be desperate, presumably for money. Henry knows every player in the fighting game. Desperate people stand out."

"Making them a perfect pressure point," Ronan added, the warm weight of his arm coaxing her to lean against him. "The question is how this links to the Shades."

"There has to be a connection. It's the same cast of characters. That's too much coincidence."

Something between apprehension and admiration flickered across Ronan's face. "Do you want me to come with you?"

"It might be better if I talked to Henry alone. He doesn't know you."

"Then I will rest a while. It takes energy to maintain a solid form for many hours."

Alana couldn't stop a smile. Ronan had been very solid on multiple occasions last night. "Sweet dreams."

Ronan leaned over, giving her one last soft kiss. Then, with a flicker of light, he dissolved into a sparkling cloud that flew toward the lamp on the bookshelf. It was fascinating to watch, but it was an uncomfortable reminder of his situation.

The lamp was the one puzzle piece that didn't fit anywhere. Ronan had called himself a weapon. From what she'd overheard, Tyrell was pressuring Corby to find the lamp because the Shades wanted it back. Somehow, Ronan was central to the whole story.

How? Why? She'd asked Ronan, but he couldn't give her answers—at least not in so many words.

She wanted to lie by his side for hours, feeling the steady beat of his heart next to hers. Alana had longed for someone to hold— and to hold her—just the way he'd done. That was a gift she'd never expected.

Surely there had to be a way to free him! She was a warrior, wasn't she?

Yes, it was easy to be brave in the comfort of her Ronan-warmed bed. With a faint groan, she rolled out of her nest and shuffled to the bathroom. She turned the shower on hot, stepped in, and let it ease away the aches from yesterday's attack. After washing, she got dressed and made coffee. She was as ready as she'd get to take on the world.

Scooping up her shoulder bag, she headed for the door, but then paused to study the lamp where it sat on the bookshelf, half-hidden by scruffy spider plants. The lamp wasn't in any obvious danger, but she didn't like the idea of leaving Ronan unguarded— not while the likes of Blacktongue and Barleycorn were sniffing around. After picking it up, she buried it in the bottom of her roomy shoulder bag, immediately feeling better.

With a genie on board, she could do anything, right?

❧ 10 ❧

Henry's gym was in a nondescript warehouse in the industrial district of town. The building didn't look like much, but it sat above the underground arena where the fights were held. The shabby paint and cracked windows on the outside provided camouflage that kept curious humans away.

As Alana had predicted, her old coach was in his lair, bellowing at the next upcoming hopeful. "Get your tail in gear, you shiftless sack of fur," Henry growled, clapping his hands so loudly the sound bounced off the high ceiling.

The unfortunate trainee—a werewolf from the big-boned look of him—jerked to attention, then ran and leaped, executing a perfect somersault midair. He landed, sprang over a vaulting horse, then ran a few steps up the wall before springing into a back-flip.

"You didn't stick the landing," Henry roared. "Do it right this time."

Alana winced in sympathy. She knew the drill. Had done it herself a thousand times. Henry never settled just for brute strength or even speed, but counted agility as an essential survival skill when it came to the fights. That was where Tina had excelled.

Alana hung back, watching for another minute. The familiar scent of resin and sweat filled the air. Somewhere, an insect buzzed lazily in the morning sunlight. It seemed as if time had stood still. Same drills, same lessons to learn, same old Henry. Sadness seeped in, along with a vague sense of betrayal. A few months ago, he'd been yelling at her and Tina. Now it was someone Alana didn't even know.

She opened her mouth to protest, but then closed it. She'd come to do a job, and needed to focus on that. Hitching her shoulder bag higher, she approached Henry with a touch of her old swagger. "Hey, Coach. What's up?"

He turned her way in surprise, but then a smile spread across his battered face. "Alana, babe." He spread his hands out. "The Incorruptible, as I live and breathe."

They hugged hard, and then he examined her. "You're a lot better," he said, sounding mystified. "You're not limping at all."

"I've been doing the exercises you gave me," she lied. "They've helped a lot."

He brightened. "Great to hear! What can I do for you?"

"I have some questions."

"About what?" The light in his eyes dimmed to suspicion. He'd always been able to read her mood.

"This and that."

Henry turned to his trainee, who was toweling the sweat from his neck. "Take ten, willya?"

"Sure thing." The young fighter turned toward the locker room with a weary hobble.

"You're riding the kid hard," Alana said.

"He's got talent." Henry put an arm around her shoulders. "So I've heard you've got a great job now, working for the young chief."

"Yup." That was what the rank and file called Tyrell. "Some

things have come up there. They've reminded me I've still got questions about my last fight."

"There's nothing new I can tell you." He said it too quickly.

"Then maybe you can tell me something old, like how long Martigen has been using gambling revenue to pay off his investor."

Henry went chalk-white. "Keep your voice down!"

He steered her toward the back corner of the gym, where there was no possibility they could be overheard. Alana followed quietly. For once, Henry was listening instead of brushing her off.

"I was with Tyrell Martigen yesterday when he was attacked by Shades," she whispered. "Or their lackeys, anyway."

"I heard." Henry's jaw bulged with tension. "What do you think I can tell you?"

Frustration itched like poison under her skin. "I heard Hugo and Tyrell talking. Are the Shades squeezing the exiled fae for gold?"

Shock blossomed across his face, as if she'd broken a rule. She held up her hands in surrender. "I wouldn't ask, but they nearly killed us."

His answer was brief. "Yes."

"Are they after all the fae?"

"The rich ones. For now."

"Why?"

His gaze slid around the room, searching for something—or someone—who wasn't there. "Have you heard the expression that an army marches on its stomach? Provisions cost money."

She folded her arms, confused. "Those things *shop*?"

Henry's expression was grim as he bent forward, keeping his voice low. "You can't *always* kill the peasants. Someone has to do the work. In many cases, a cash transaction is the simple answer."

Alana stared at the scarred wooden floor without really seeing it. "They get money from this realm through the mirrors and into their pockets?"

He nodded. "Gold and rubies spend most places."

"Who would deal with them? A lot of fae remember the invasion."

"You'd be surprised. Blackmail. Threats against a child or a lover. People cave."

Their eyes met. Her gut said he was telling the truth.

"What have they got to do with Martigen Industries?" she whispered.

"Everything funnels through Martigen." Henry jerked his chin at the gym. "Like I said, they need the money. I've put two and two together, just like you."

It was as she'd suspected. If the Shades wanted funds to support their next conquest, the underground fights made money flow like nothing else. Even the mayor was sending fat envelopes to Tyrell, the bookmaker with the magic mirror in his front hall.

Alana spun, savagely kicking the wall. The so-called investor wasn't an investor at all, but a leech sucking the life blood of the exiled fae community. And sooner or later, some fool would open the door and let them in, giving the Shades a whole new world to destroy.

Alana felt the heat climbing up her cheeks. She clutched the strap of her shoulder bag like a comfort object. "Our fight was fixed for a big payoff, wasn't it?"

Henry's face was haggard. "I swear by the Wheel I didn't know that was going to happen."

"But you knew something!"

"They asked me who would win." Henry looked away. "I told them no one could beat you."

He'd finally admitted it. She should have felt relief, but instead a sour burn hurt her stomach.

He touched her arm, bridging the gulf that suddenly yawned between them. "I swear I didn't know you were in danger. I never would have let you walk into the circle if I had."

"Who did it?" she ground out.

"I don't know who did the poisoning."

"Was it you?"

"No!" His voice rose, and he visibly struggled to rein in his temper. "I swear to you, no."

Maybe that was true, but Tina was dead and the enemy was on the doorstep. She was tempted, so very tempted, to use a wish to get the answers out of him. Something told her, though, that Henry would never forgive such a violation of his will.

"What am I supposed to do with this?" she asked, pulling out of his reach. "Fighters have been dying these last couple of years. Is this a pattern?"

"Stay out of it, Alana," Henry warned. "If not for your own sake, for the rest of us. Most of us have something to lose."

No, most people weren't like her, a girl whose adopted family had given up on their talentless daughter. Most people didn't have friends who died on the packed dirt of a basement arena. Lucky them. Now her coach stood before her, telling her to let the enemy win. Disappointment tightened around her ribs. "Don't you want to fight back?" she demanded. "For Tina?"

He shook his head. "There's no answer I can give that you'll like. These people don't make empty threats. Trust me on that one."

Somehow, Alana found her smile. It felt cold and hard on her lips. "You taught me to fight, Henry. Too late to regret that now."

With that, she stalked out, letting the heavy fire door slam behind her.

She fished her sunglasses out of her bag and slid them on, blinking back tears. Physical pain never made her cry, but this had hurt her heart. Henry was her friend, her mentor, but he'd given in. It would have been easier if she could have hated him, but he had family to protect.

She'd loathed the Shades before, but in a theoretical way. Now they'd stolen her faith in her friend.

Halfway down the block, she caught a glimpse of movement

near one of the neighboring warehouses. She backtracked a few steps, searching the corners and loading bays, but saw nothing. After a few fruitless moments, she moved on, but the nagging sense of trouble didn't leave her. She slipped into a deep doorway, using its shade for cover.

"What's wrong?"

She spun, bumping into the warmth of Ronan's chest. "I spoke to Henry. You wouldn't believe…"

"I heard it all." Giving her a slight smile, he squeezed her hand. "The lamp is in your bag, remember?"

"I thought Henry had our backs."

"I'm sure he is doing what he can."

She realized how much she craved Ronan's touch right then, and threaded her fingers through his.

Ronan stroked her cheek, his touch impossibly gentle. His carefulness was still a surprise to her—so many men never saw beyond her strength. "Why did you stop here?" he asked.

"I had a bad feeling." She studied his face, the memories of last night overlaid with the mystery of who and what he was. And why did caution melt away every time he got close?

She pulled her wits together, catching motion from the corner of her eye. Henry was leaving the gym, striding in the opposite direction. "I wonder where he's going in such a hurry?"

Ronan raised a brow. "Might I suggest we follow? You stay behind him. I will look ahead."

With that, he dissolved into smoke, leaving her alone. Alana waited until Henry turned the corner, then ran across the street to fall into step a block behind him. She hadn't got halfway before someone else emerged from an alleyway further ahead. It was Randall, the sleazy job applicant who was now working for Hugo Martigen. Alana's stomach flipped with apprehension. Was it Randall she'd seen lurking nearby? He seemed like a lurking kind of guy.

He reached the corner first, vanishing quickly. She doubled

her pace, wanting to catch up before she lost the two men. As she drew near, she heard voices.

"Is that why you called me all the way out here?" Henry asked, loud and unhappy. "Is this your big emergency? Grab some brains!"

She slowed, hugging the wall so she could peer around the corner unseen. Henry stood outside a small neighborhood coffee shop that had tables and chairs on the sidewalk. A few of the early bird locals were drinking coffee, eating pastries, and watching Henry lose his temper. Randall was walking up to him, but he wasn't the one the coach was bellowing at. Alana leaned a bit further, catching a glimpse of Corby standing with his hands on his hips.

So Corby had summoned Henry. Alana hadn't known they were even acquainted. She hung back, wanting to hear more.

"It *is* an emergency, Blackwell," Corby said. He sat on one of the metal bistro chairs before placing something on the table. Alana couldn't tell what it was until it moved.

A bug. Fae listening devices were actual insects, although they spoke in a language trained handlers could understand. This one looked about the size of her palm, although it was hard to tell from a distance. Was that what she'd sensed lurking around?

One by one, the humans were picking up their coffee mugs and phones and preparing to go. They couldn't see the bug—that would be hidden from their sight—but even Alana could feel the push of a repulsion spell designed to send potential witnesses on their way. Before a minute was up, the three fae men were alone.

"What did he tell the she-devil?" Randall asked Corby. His tone said he hadn't forgiven her for the incident in Barleycorn's office.

"My former employee seemed to know a great deal before she got there. Blackwell filled in a few blanks."

Why are they bugging Henry? Bewildered, Alana leaned against the side of the building, grateful for its support.

"For shame," Corby said. "I thought our coach here understood discretion."

"I do," Henry replied. "She just showed up. I had no idea she was coming."

Guilt hammered Alana, turning her stomach sour. *This is my fault!*

"A nosy creature, isn't she?" Corby slipped the bug into his shirt pocket. It crawled in until nothing but the long antennae showed. "It's not your job to satisfy her curiosity. It's your job to make sure the fights go our way."

"I've told you before, I won't put my fighters in danger."

Corby snapped his fingers, and a privacy shield snapped into place around them. They were invisible and inaudible to anyone but fae. They might be right outside the coffee shop playing a brass band, but no humans would know.

"Shoulda played dumb," Randall said sadly.

Henry's face went red. "And you're volunteering to give lessons?"

Randall shifted his stance, spreading his feet apart, and cracked his knuckles. "Sure, I'll teach you a lesson."

Alana nearly rolled her eyes. This had to stop. She hitched her bag so the strap sat securely across her body, then stepped into view. "Howdy boys, I do believe my ears are burning."

Randall's eyes went round with surprise. Then he pulled a gun. It figured he'd take the lazy way out rather than train with knives like every other fae warrior.

Henry grabbed for the weapon. Alana watched in horror as the two men wrestled over the firearm, sure someone was going to be shot. Meanwhile, Corby spun to make his escape, but Ronan blocked his path. As the genie had promised, he'd gone ahead of Henry and now cut off that escape route.

Alana caught up to Randall, immediately kicking the gun out of his hand. The weapon flew harmlessly away, but the impact loosened Henry's grip on the man. Randall tried to bolt, but

Alana delivered an elbow square to his chest. He reeled back, almost falling into Henry's arms, before the coach socked him in the jaw. Randall dropped like a stone.

Alana picked up the gun, then handed it to Henry. "He's all yours."

Henry nodded, not meeting her eyes, but squeezed her hand as he took the weapon. He aimed the gun at Randall's head.

Just then, an unholy screech tore the area. The first thing Alana saw was the surveillance bug streaking through the air as if every bat and bird had declared it lunch. Then she caught sight of Corby. He'd been trying to get past Ronan, but the genie was too quick—so the crusty old bookseller was coming apart. Literally.

First, a seam opened from the crown of his head down the entire midline of his body. Then, like the covers of a book, the two halves of Corby folded back. A black mass spilled out. It began unfurling, plumping and filling out as each piece found room. It grew taller than Corby—at least twice his size—and rose on two scaled legs. Twin blades, curved and sharp and shining black, pushed out, growing longer and longer.

"What is that thing?" Alana asked in horror as she backed away.

They had to stop it, but how? There was nothing left of Corby now—not the Corby she knew. In its place was a dark and shaggy heap of—feathers?

With blinding speed, Corby snapped at Ronan, his great beak clacking. It closed on smoke. A second later, Ronan was at Alana's side, his body poised and ready to fight. Then the thing hunched, swinging its head around to find its prey. Alana had never screamed in her life, but this time she came close. That beak could slice a limb in two.

The black eyes were Corby's, with all the man's sharp intelligence. And now, they were filled with an equal measure of malice. It was an expression she'd never expected to see on a bird, even a crow ten feet tall.

But damn it, that was still her former boss. She stabbed a finger his way. "You traitor!"

The bird stretched its black wings and cawed, a raucous, ear-splitting torture that had them covering their ears. Corby struck again, his beak grazing Alana's arm as it pecked for the bag holding the lamp.

Henry fired the gun, and black feathers sprayed around them. With a ragged shriek, Corby sprang into the air, flapping wildly. Henry shot again, daring Corby to getting any closer. With a final filthy glare, the bird straightened his course and headed north.

The shield around them dissolved. Someone across the street stopped, pointing at Randall's downed form. Alana cursed. That was all they needed—helpful bystanders.

"Corby went for the lamp," Alana said to Ronan. "He knows we have it—he probably smelled it in my bag. We have to stop him before he reports back to his mirror."

Ronan had gone pale. She knew no one needed to tell him what could go wrong if that happened. "He's going in the direction of his shop."

"How do we catch him?"

Ronan paused, thoughts chasing across his face. "Hang on a moment." He ran into the coffee shop.

Henry looked from Alana to Ronan, then pressed the gun into Alana's hand. "If you're going after Corby, take this. You don't want to get close to that thing."

"What about you?" Alana asked, surveying the street for more onlookers.

"I'll call my student to come help me with this fool." Henry gave Randall a casual kick.

Alana examined the weapon. Guns weren't her first choice, but the bullets had hurt Corby. That was good enough for her. "Thank you," she said, pressing Henry's arm.

Ronan emerged from the shop dragging a worn bit of carpet scattered with crumbs. "It's not much, but it will do."

"Do for what?" Alana asked, mystified.

"Come here," he said. "Quickly."

Obediently, she ran to where he stood in the middle of the threadbare rug. She could see dents in the pile where table legs had sat. She wondered what Ronan had done to convince the cafe owner to give it up.

"Sit," he said, pulling her down beside him. "Hang on tight."

She was about to protest when she felt the earth shift beneath her. Speechless, she grabbed for the fringed edge of the carpet with her gun-free hand. When the thing shot straight upward, she finally let loose a scream.

"Apologies." Ronan clearly found the moment funny even though he put a comforting arm around her waist. "This one's a bit of a beater."

"Ronan," she growled between clenched teeth. Below she could see a gobsmacked Henry craning his neck while he talked on his phone.

And then the carpet swept through the air after the monstrous crow. She clenched her teeth, trying to ignore the tiny moans of dismay coming from her throat. Scrunching her eyes closed, she hugged her shoulder bag close. Alana wouldn't look down. She couldn't, or she'd be sick for sure. She'd faced down all manner of monsters, but she'd done it with her feet on the ground. This was a new kind of awful.

But not for Ronan. She could feel it along the long, hot line where her body touched his. While she was as stiff as a board, his muscles were loose, flexing easily with the movement of the air. Curiosity dared her to open her eyes, but she restricted herself to looking at him. She could only see his profile, but that was enough to know he was in his element. His eyes were closed to slits, and a faint smile played around his lips as he leaned into the wind.

"You *like* this," she said, her tone scandalized. She had to shout to be heard above the rush of wind.

He laughed, the wild glee in it saying more than any words. Alana swallowed hard. Air fae. They had a reputation for being just a little crazy. Of course, she was the one who'd gotten herself into this mess. Blasting through the air on a scatter rug wasn't the mark of a responsible adult.

Alana huffed an exasperated breath, hating that she was so afraid. Well, if he could stand this, so could she. Forcing her gaze down, she shivered. She was apprehensive, but she was also frozen by the chill breeze whipping around her body. Grimly, she leaned forward an inch to get a better view.

And forgot everything else. The city spread out below, sparkling in the morning sun. Despite their altitude, Alana's heart skipped at the unexpected beauty of it. The city's two bridges spanned the inlet, cars streaming across them like slithering strings of beads. Buildings thrust upward beneath them, barely recognizable from this angle. They skimmed the rooftops, dodging in and out of their massive shadows as the carpet found the quickest route.

They were flying as the crow flew. She could see Corby ahead and below, a giant black mass moving far faster than any ordinary bird. They were pacing him, but would need to speed up to catch him before he reached the shop. Alana didn't want to face Corby on his own ground, with all those magical toys lurking in his office safe—not to mention that blasted mirror. He'd have an arsenal on his side.

They'd have to confront him in the air. She'd have to shoot him. Her stomach rolled at the thought. Fighting was one thing— as brutal as it was, she never set out to kill anyone. As she'd told Barleycorn, she'd only accept an honest job. But saving the world from Shades surely counted.

She spotted Comfy Chair's neighborhood in the distance. "Can this thing go any faster?"

Ronan nodded, then the carpet tilted as it caught the updraft between buildings. Alana squeaked, her death grip on the carpet fringe tightening another notch, but she didn't slide off. Whatever magic made the thing fly apparently kept its passengers secure.

They angled over a street, using the office buildings as visual cover while Ronan closed the distance. The excitement of the chase rolled off him like a scent. Her own pulse sped in sympathy, and she dared to release her hold of the carpet fringe to ready a two-handed grip on the gun.

Their flight took them over a familiar part of the downtown, all but strafing a rooftop volleyball game before swooping beneath the glassed-in walkway that stretched between two towers. She knew Ronan was using some sort of charm to hide them from human eyes. But then they streaked past the building where the Wildwood Agency had its offices. She caught a glimpse of Barleycorn standing at his window, and by the startled turn of his head, she knew they had been seen.

She cursed, but decided to face that problem once they'd dealt with Corby. There was a break between the buildings where the street ended in a park, and she saw they'd drawn neck and neck with the crow. She finally had a clean shot. As if in response to her wishes, the carpet steadied. She aimed and fired.

And missed. She was better with knives.

"Argh!" she cried in frustration, but Ronan was already circling for another attempt. The park ended, and their sightline was again broken by flashing walls of glass as they sped past high-rises. He spiraled up for better visibility—only for them to see that Corby had vanished.

They paused in the air only for a fraction of a second, then Ronan dropped into a steep dive. Alana's breath stopped as her flesh resisted the sudden pull of gravity. It was horrifying, crushing, but when she managed to look up, she understood the move. Corby had somehow come behind them, and was hot on their tail. Alana's vision filled with the gigantic beak opening to reveal a blue-black tongue. She swung the gun up, intending to send a bullet right down its gaping throat, and tried to ignore the ground rushing up to meet them.

Ronan chose that moment for evasive maneuvers. The carpet pulled out of the dive with stomach-churning speed, and Alana grabbed for the carpet again. Corby flapped wildly, the huge wings thundering as he tried to slow his descent. With their quarry stalled, Ronan sent the carpet in a graceful loop—upside down—over the bird. For the second time that day, Alana screamed and clutched her bag so the lamp didn't come tumbling out.

And then the sky was above them once more, and Corby was ahead. Alana aimed and fired. This time, the bullet scored deeply along the crow's flank. Black feathers sailed through the air, twirling as they fell.

Corby strained forward, now flying for his life. The store was just one street over. They had seconds to catch up—but something new was happening. The air above Comfy Chair Books and Collectibles was growing solid. No, that wasn't right. It was growing *reflective*, casting back images of the sky and buildings around them so the space above the store seemed to fold back on itself.

"He's using the mirror in his office," Ronan shouted. "He's summoned the Shimmer."

He was about to get away. "Faster!" she cried.

The carpet shot forward, as if using all the genie's strength and will. Alana crouched, making herself more aerodynamic, and sighted on the crow. The second before she pulled the trigger, Corby vanished.

He'd been there.

Now he wasn't.

The Shimmer was gone, too. The carpet whooshed over the store as if Corby and his magic had never been there. Alana snarled, a sound of frustration beyond words. They'd lost him. Now the Shades would find out about the lamp, and the Wheel only knew what they'd do to get Ronan back.

Or what they'd do to Ronan once they had him.

Alana sank back on her heels, hot tears of frustration tracking down her cheeks. "I wish we knew where Corby went!"

Ronan flinched as if someone had punched him in the gut.

She clapped a hand over her mouth, but it was too late. Her second wish was made, whether she'd planned to use it this way or not.

The world went utterly black and cold—so very cold. Blind and freezing, she grabbed for Ronan's hand, and was relieved to find it was there. She had a wild thought they'd followed Corby into death.

And then they were back in the world, but instead of the city, she gazed over a rugged landscape of scrub and rock, split by a wide brown river. Ronan made a strangled noise. The thick muscles of his forearms flexed as he gripped the carpet, and it began to descend.

Alana opened her mouth to object. A piece of her brain was still fixated on chasing Corby, but he was nowhere in sight. Maybe this was where he'd gone, but her wish hadn't been any more specific than that. Nothing guaranteed they'd actually catch him.

The rug landed with a bump. Ronan sprang from it, running a dozen steps to stare out at the stark landscape. Alana unfolded herself, amazed at how stiff she'd become. Magic carpets were anything but ergonomic.

She walked to Ronan's side. It seemed they'd landed on a plain of scrubby grass. Ahead, a river valley dipped away. The surrounding rock formations were striated in shades of red and orange, reminding her a bit of the Grand Canyon. As the freezing cold from the ride left her body, she realized the temperature was sweltering.

He suddenly turned and folded her in his arms, his grip intense, almost crushing. Alana struggled to read his mood, but couldn't figure it out. "What's going on?" she asked gently.

By way of reply, he kissed her long and hard. His touch was searching, but it wasn't the prelude to intimacy. It was deeply personal in another way.

The moment he released her, he sank to his knees and braced his palms on the ground. She knelt beside him. "What is it?"

He shook his head, grabbing up a handful of the rust-colored soil. It trickled through his fingers, sending up a tiny cloud of dust. "This is more than I could have ever hoped for."

"What?" She was getting impatient to understand.

"My most excellent warrior, you made that wish for us both." His eyes bright, he grinned. "This is my home."

❧ 12 ❧

Well, this was new.

If Ronan was home, they were in the faery realm. Alana hadn't planned to hop between realities when she'd set out that morning. Or ever. Panic began bubbling deep inside. How on earth was she going to get back?

She spun, taking in the landscape one more time. This time, she saw evidence of people in the distance—tiny pockets of activity, as if farmers were just gaining a toehold. Clusters of animal pens and brick-and-thatch houses were tucked deep into the river valley. Tilled green fields spread like a rising flush beside the water, an indication of careful irrigation. "I didn't know so many fae stayed here rather than going into exile."

"Bright Wing did not go into exile. Nor did their tenants. At least, not all of them." He pointed toward the settlements. "I see they are trying to rebuild."

"Are they safe?"

"I can only assume the Shades have moved on to find more interesting victims." His mouth set in a grim line. "They could reduce all this to ash if they chose."

"You mean maybe the Evil Empire's sudden interest in the human realm is giving these folks a chance to recover?"

"Maybe."

"Talk about a good news, bad news situation." She tried to think past the mental voice screaming that she was stuck in an alien universe. "Look, we need to get out of the open. Corby will have gone straight to Shade HQ, and they'll call out the dogs as soon as they hear we're on this side of the Shimmer. Should I wish us back?"

"No!" He cast her a stern look. "Don't use your wish for that."

"You want to stay here?"

"Yes, but that is not the reason."

She considered. "Is it bad luck to undo one wish with another?"

His face shuttered, as if hiding an internal struggle. "It rarely works out as expected. Trust me on this."

Alana nodded in reluctant agreement. "Then what should we do? It's going to be a lot harder to stop Corby now."

"I need to get you to safety. That means another flight, but a short one this time."

He sounded so protective she had to smile. "You're the one the Shades want, not me."

"You've defied them, interfered with their plans, and attacked one of their servants." He ran a proprietary hand down her arm, as if he were proud of what she'd done. "They will demand retribution."

"Good times."

Alana took her place on the carpet. They rose high into the cloudless sky, and she felt the full force of the bright, hot sun as they flew toward the distant mountains. The density of the little farms increased until they melded into a city built from the same yellowish brick.

"What's that?" she asked.

"Kyleen, the capital of Bright Wing's lands."

"Did you live here?" she asked.

"Not quite. Near here, though."

Kyleen wasn't like anyplace Alana had ever seen. From the air, she could see the streets were laid out like the spokes of a wheel radiating from a central plaza. Oxen pulled carts along the wide thoroughfares, passing open markets and public wells. Judging from the piles of rubble across the city, very few of the major buildings still stood.

The destruction sobered Alana. What damage could the Shades do if they reached her world? What if they learned to use human technology? Human weapons?

The carpet changed direction, angling north to pick up a faster air current. Slowly, they gained altitude. Ronan pointed to the left. "Do you see that flat-topped mountain?"

"Yes." Something about its shape seemed familiar.

"That is the Wheel, where High King Jorwarth once sat upon the throne. The kings are dead, the council scattered, but someday from the ashes will rise the flame. We have sworn it."

Alana's mouth fell open. She was staring at the real-life version of the tapestry Barleycorn had hanging in his office. Unexpectedly reverent, she took it all in. The Wheel was the hearthstone of the fae identity, a symbol of unity among the tribes. Gripping Ronan's shoulder, she pointed. "I want to go back and see that up close!"

"Later," he said. "I promise."

"Where are we going now?"

"I'm taking you to my old home. We should be safe there."

Ronan's home? Alana's stomach fluttered with curiosity and misgivings. "Can you do that? As a genie, I mean?"

He shook his head, brows drawn. "I don't know how things will be. I have not returned there since the war."

Alana did the math. That meant centuries had passed, which was further complicated by the fact that time moved differently between realms. From Ronan's perspective, his absence might have been even longer. Fae were immortal, but that did not mean they were endlessly resilient.

What would his friends and family think of his return? What sort of welcome would he get? Who was to say his home was still there?

They went deeper into the range, passing crag after crag until Alana had no sense of how long they'd been flying. After time, one wild vista appeared much like the next—at least to a city girl like her. Eventually—finally—Ronan guided the carpet toward a castle of gray stone so dark it was nearly black. Alana peered at the massive pile, her eyes dry from the wind in her face. The place had clearly seen battle. The massive gatehouse was missing a corner of its tower, and one of the tall spires behind it was crumbled altogether. Still, smoke rose here and there, giving signs that someone was home.

Ronan guided the carpet up and up, passing over the front of the castle to the mountain behind. It was then Alana saw that the towers were carved from the rock face itself, making Ronan's old home as much part of the mountain as its forest and ice-laden peak.

A crag hung over the castle like a frowning brow crusted with icicles and stunted pines. Along its length crouched an *enormous* gray dragon. It was the biggest living thing Alana had ever seen, with softly shining scales that were as broad as dinner plates. Its huge, wedge-shaped head reared up as they approached, poised on a snakelike neck ridged with bony plates down its spine. At the sight of it—the great orange eyes and backswept horns—Alana forgot to breathe.

Barleycorn had implied the dragons were dead. He'd clearly been wrong.

The carpet touched down at the creature's feet. Ronan leaped up before sweeping into a low bow. Thinking it best to follow his lead, Alana did the same. The dragon's snout lowered, tendrils of smoke drifting from the wide nostrils. It sniffed Ronan, then

Alana, but immediately returned to the genie. Then it gave a low, almost keening growl before butting Ronan with its nose. The gesture was affectionate, but also demanding.

Ronan straightened, then bent his head in a show of respect. "Hello, Father."

Father? Alana must have made a noise, because both males turned her way. *Ronan is a dragon!* She'd guessed he was an air fae, but this was beyond her wildest imaginings.

The implications crowded her mind. The great winged beasts were, literally and figuratively, at the very apex of the fae food chain. How, by the Wheel, had the Shades imprisoned *a dragon?* Her estimation of their power went up another frightening degree.

"Father, may I present to you Alana Beech?"

Alana made her best bow. Henry had taught her a few manners, along with how to punch someone in the throat. "I am honored, sir."

The dragon huffed softly.

"Forgive my father's lack of conversation," a female voice said. "He has vowed to keep constant vigil over the land, so he remains in his beast form."

Alana looked over her shoulder to see a tall, dark-haired young woman standing in front of a heavy oak door that was set into the rock. Her gown of yellow silk fell in pleats to the ground. The silver-trimmed sleeves had a wide, bell-like hem that reached her knees and gave every gesture a look of measured elegance. The eyes that searched Alana's face were the same near-black as Ronan's.

"Fliss!" Ronan exclaimed. His features froze, as if hiding uncertainty, and he remained poised mid-step until the young woman opened her arms. Then he rushed into her embrace, lifting her feet from the ground.

"So, big brother, where have you been?" she asked lightly.

"Nowhere I treasured so much as home."

And then Fliss burst into tears, as sudden as a summer storm. "Oh, Ronan, you great wandering idiot, you wouldn't believe what it's been like here! I've needed you so much." Her wrenching sobs tore a hole in Alana's heart.

With a loud scrabbling, the dragon slid from the ledge and sailed out of sight with one thundering beat of wings. Evidently, he had no patience for tearful reunions.

In contrast, Ronan held his sister close, letting the sobs gradually quiet. When the two finally broke apart, Ronan seemed shaken. "I'm sorry, Fliss."

"Where were you?" she said with an angry sniff.

"In the human realm."

"How did you get there for pity's sake?"

Alana held her breath, unsure what Ronan would say. His eyes met hers, and she saw the question written there. Alana nodded. She would go along with whatever path he took. This was his family.

"Forgive me, Fliss," Ronan began. "I will not tell you a lie, but I'm not ready to tell you everything that has happened. Ask me no questions, I beg you."

Fliss's pretty face filled with disappointment, then suspicion. "Why not?"

"Because that is the only way I can remain."

Fliss stood very still, her fingers curled into fists. Alana could almost see her thoughts—how she needed Ronan there, loved him, but didn't understand his secrets. Eventually, she took a breath and tossed back her hair. "I'll allow you a reprieve, brother, since you've just returned. But you owe me one answer right away."

Ronan's brows lowered in a frown. "What would that be?"

"You were gone forever," Fliss said, defiance in her tone. "How did you get home again?"

Ronan relaxed. "Alana was born on the other side of the Shimmer. She brought me back. Don't ask her how she did it."

Fliss's dark gaze flicked her way. Alana repeated her bow, feeling windblown and grubby beside the beautifully dressed female. Ronan and Fliss were clearly aristocrats, far above her in rank and wealth.

"Then welcome to Highclaw Castle." Ronan's sister held out both hands. "And thank you for returning this rogue to us. I am Fliss, the troublesome younger sister."

That surprised a laugh from Alana. "I'm very pleased to meet you."

"Come inside," Fliss said, gesturing to the oak door. "Unless, Ronan, you'd like to stay behind and fly patrol with Father?"

Ronan glanced at Alana, a flash of panic in his eyes. Alana connected the dots—if he could have changed into dragon form, he would have. Corby—and everyone else who annoyed him—would have become an afternoon snack. The loss of his beast form was something he didn't want his family to know. They had to improvise.

"I'm afraid that's not possible," Alana said, taking Ronan's arm possessively. "I'm afraid he takes after his father, at least in terms of making vows."

"Oh?" Fliss arched an eyebrow, curiosity plain on her face. "And what vow would that be?"

Ronan's expression said he was wondering as well. Alana's mind blanked. "Um—he vowed he'd stay in this handsome form until," she hesitated, smiling brightly to cover her confusion, "until I agree to marry him."

He gave a slight hiss of breath, so soft she only heard it because she stood so close. Marry him? By the Wheel, where had that come from? Oh right, one of those romance novels at the store. She lowered her eyes, not wanting to see Ronan's face just in case she broke into panicked giggles. *He's a dragon, and I just threatened to marry him!* No doubt he was regretting ever leaving his lamp.

The thought summoned a rush of mortification. Alana's

cheeks heated, but she straightened her spine to meet whatever came next.

"You're making him wait," Fliss said. "Good for you. I can't wait to hear the details."

Details?

Ronan cleared his throat. "It's a work in progress."

Fliss smiled, but Alana couldn't tell how real that expression was.

They passed through the oak door into a vaulted hallway carved into the mountain. Fliss led them down a spiral staircase that led to the main tower of the castle. Broad hallways, high and wide enough for an adult dragon, criss-crossed between vast, ornate chambers.

If the outside of Castle Highclaw was dark and rough, the inside was its opposite. Everything was light and spacious. Pale marble lined the floor, while whimsical frescoes covered the ceilings with birds, butterflies, and endless sunlight. Tall windows glowed with panes of colored glass, and artwork hung in gold-leafed frames. Alana had heard stories of dragons and their hoards, but she hadn't imagined their dens quite like this. It was like walking through a kaleidoscope of jewels.

And then there were the people in the castle. Tidings of Ronan's return spread with wildfire speed even as they walked, as if whispers traveled faster than their feet. Clearly Fliss wasn't the only one happy to see him, because the news was greeted with shouts of happiness and applause wherever they passed. Many of the castle residents were tall like Fliss and Ronan, their features similar enough Alana guessed they were also dragons. Others had horns, wings, or other markings that showed they were from different fae tribes. Most striking were the tall young warriors who bowed low enough to sweep the ground. Alana overheard their whispers.

"The son of the dragon has returned. I bet he's going to clean house."

"Ronan is back. Now the Shades will pay."

"He led us to victory before. He'll do it again."

They entered a salon filled with tables and chairs. It seemed to be a gathering place for military officers, both old and young, who played chess or sprawled in comfortable armchairs, holding goblets of wine.

"Greetings, gentlemen," Ronan called out as he barged in, cutting conversation off with one sharp glance. "If you would follow me, I would like a word."

Some stood instantly, others with reluctance or confusion on their faces. One continued to snore until Ronan prodded him with a foot. He snorted awake, astonishment evident, and jumped to his feet. "General!" Then he bowed. "My prince."

Prince? Alana stopped in her tracks. Apparently sensing her sudden dismay, Ronan turned and took her hand, but she didn't budge. *Ronan was the Prince of Bright Wing? That dragon outside is King Vass!*

"What's wrong?" he asked in a murmur.

"You're a prince," she whispered.

"And I'm yours to command." He tugged her forward. "Come on. These people are expecting a show."

One after another, the warriors fell into step behind Ronan, swelling their small party until a mob filled the castle's echoing corridor. Alana's wits scattered like a flock of pigeons, but she began to pick up on details—that some faces registered resentment of Ronan's return, that cobwebs clung in corners, and there was a general air of chaos.

She leaned close to Ronan. "Is there a queen?"

His face tightened. "No. Dragons mate for life, and my mother passed during the war."

Alana had never been to a royal court, but she understood pack behavior. With the king dedicated to his vigil and no queen in residence, keeping order wouldn't be easy. No wonder Fliss had been overjoyed to see her brother home.

Ronan led the growing entourage into a massive hall where two thrones sat upon a carved dais. He ran up the steps of the dais to stand before them, his feet apart as if to challenge any who dared to question his place. In a moment, he'd made the shift from prodigal son to future monarch. The entire company fell to one knee—some fast, some slow, but there was none who defied him. Alana knelt with everyone else, impressed by Ronan's ability to dominate the crowd with his presence.

"As you can see, I'm back," Ronan said after a long moment of silence. "I see some familiar faces, old friends, and a handful I regard as teachers and second fathers. But there are many new ones as well. Brave generations have risen to pick up the swords of those who fell during the conquest."

A cheer went up from the young men, and the hair rose along Alana's scalp. As different as these fae of the air were from Alana, she knew fighters. Beneath the shout, she could hear the roar of battle.

"In the years of my absence, I heard tell of the many defeats of my people, of the valiant defense by the fire fae, and of the terrible losses of the merfolk of the Outward Isles. The Wheel stands bare, a grave with nothing but wind and ashes. We could not blame the stranger who believes the Kingdom of Faery is lost."

The room was perfectly silent. Not even the sound of breathing disturbed the expectant quiet.

"But we are not lost," Ronan said, his voice rising with defiance. "Bright Wing defends the last fae kingdom of the Wheel! Our brothers and sisters of the earth, fire, and water will see our defiance and remember their freedom! We shall light the beacon atop the Wheel, and call the high king back to his throne!"

Another roar shook Alana's bones. She could feel the people of the castle drinking in his words like rain after a crippling drought. Ronan had barely begun talking, but that didn't matter.

They needed a real leader. They were afraid without him. As Fliss had done, a few had burst into tears.

Swept up in the emotion, Alana cupped her hands around her mouth and whooped.

"My friends," Ronan continued, "we shall do more than hold our borders. We shall defeat the enemy. We shall break their power. Then we shall scour every last Shade from the realm!"

He thrust a fist into the air, his eyes flashing with a fury that stole Alana's breath. Her chest ached at the sight. He was a prince, no question. He held the room with an authority that only came from hard years of earning his people's respect.

He'd earned Alana's in that moment. She knew, as only a warrior could, when a leader was willing to stand and die with his troops. Yes, she would fight for him and his mission.

Except he wasn't free. She was his owner—at least until she used that third wish. His true master—the very one Ronan wanted to fight—held the chains that bound him. How, by the name of all that was fae, did Ronan plan to pull this off?

"**O**h, stuff me down a volcano and call me cooked," Fliss said to Alana after Ronan's speech was done. "You're a mess."

Alana shrugged, not sure what to say. "I can wash off in the stable yard."

"Don't be ridiculous," Fliss said, grabbing Alana's sleeve and towing her down the palace corridor. "Ronan requested I take charge of you. Believe me, when he gets that stubborn look, it's easier just to say yes. You should know that if you are to be his mate."

Fliss was slight as a reed, but she was strong. Alana was soon trailing in her wake. *His mate.* She wished she'd never mentioned marriage. "I could use something to eat," she conceded.

"Right." Fliss nodded, flipping dark curls over her shoulder. "What do you eat over on your side of the Shimmer? Are we likely to have it?"

"Just keep it simple and we should be okay."

"No whole raw goats still warm from the meadow?" Fliss grinned at Alana's expression. "The older dragons like their traditions, but I think we can rustle up some bread and cheese."

Alana was seventy percent sure Fliss was teasing.

They stopped in front of an arched door. "This is the part of the castle where the family lives," Fliss said. "This used to be my big sister's room."

"Did she move away?" Alana asked.

Fliss pressed her lips into a line. "There were nine of us children before the invasion. Now that our brother Telkoram is away on a mission, Ronan and I are the only ones left. It's just been Father and me for some time. If you truly brought Ronan home, we're forever in your debt."

Alana couldn't find words. Seeing her struggle, Fliss gave a lopsided smile. "Dragons don't give up what's theirs, regardless of the cost. Bright Wing held its land, and kept many of the farmers safe. That's why we wear the crown." Pushing the door open, she led the way inside.

Alana stopped dead, her shoulder bag dropping to the carpet. "This is far too nice for just me."

The chamber was twice as big as her apartment, with a large balcony overlooking a view of the mountains. The ceiling was painted with a flight of pastel dragons, and in the center of the room stood a large bed hung with silk curtains and mounded with pillows. It was all beautiful, and it made Alana feel in dire need of a bath.

"I could find you something in the dungeons, if you prefer," Fliss said dryly. "But it's a long flight of stairs back to the dining room."

"Sorry," Alana said. "I don't mean to sound ungrateful—truly I don't. It's just more than I'm used to."

Fliss hopped up on the bed, swinging her feet. Just for the moment, she seemed very young. "So tell me, Alana Beech of the mortal realm, what *are* you used to?"

Alana's heart twisted at Fliss's bantering tone. Her mind flashed to Tina, who'd been her only real female friend. She missed the inside jokes, the pep talks, and the junk food nights.

Alana shifted uncomfortably. "Nothing as exciting as you, I'm sure. You've been running this castle."

"Almost." Fliss fell back on the bed, staring at the ceiling. "With Father otherwise occupied, keeping order with this lot is like herding a colony of feral cats. I've got the job done, but not without a lot of hissing and scratching and spraying the furniture."

"Not literally, I hope?"

"Not quite." Fliss turned her head without sitting up. "You didn't answer my question."

"Hard work," Alana said. "I'm used to hard work."

"And you're a warrior. Ronan said so."

"Yes."

Fliss sat up, cupping her chin in her hands. "Well, then, you must have fascinating stories to tell."

Not without giving away too much, Alana thought. No doubt Fliss was genuinely interested in a visiting stranger just because, but she was also an experienced courtier. The princess would pump Alana for whatever information she could get.

Alana folded her arms. "I should be with Ronan and his soldiers."

"In good time." Fliss gave a smile that was more than part grimace. "Trust me, right now the boys are indulging in a lot of preening and boasting and sorting out who has the biggest roar. The real work will begin after everyone has settled down."

Alana tensed. How long would it be before they realized Ronan wasn't a dragon? And then what would happen? Apprehension made her heart beat faster, and Fliss lifted her head as if she could hear it.

"And me?" Alana asked. "What am I to do?"

Fliss shrugged. "Eat. Bathe. Tell me all about the human realm."

Better than letting her nerves blow their cover. "What do you want to know?"

The young dragon brightened, as if this was what she'd been waiting for. "What do people do for amusement on your side of the Shimmer? What do they wear? What music do they like?"

Alana surrendered, telling Fliss whatever she could think of, from social media to chili dogs to dating apps. Food arrived on a huge platter, and Alana feasted on chicken pie, fruit, and wine. Fliss ate with her, refusing to end her barrage of questions.

"Tell me again about these sites you speak of. You look at a male's picture to decide on his worth as a mate?"

"Not just the picture. They give some basic information about themselves."

"And then there are adoption sites for animals, which also have pictures and information?"

"Right."

Fliss wrinkled her brow. "Which do you go to in order to meet shifters?"

Alana nearly choked on her wine. Fliss began to giggle, and then all hope of intelligent conversation ended.

Servants brought hot water for a bath and a selection of clothes. Fliss helped Alana comb the tangles from her hair, then assisted her in buttoning in a pale green gown. It was a similar style to the one Fliss wore, with a V-shaped neck and dangling sleeves. This one had gathers just beneath Alana's breasts, highlighting her feminine shape. It was the most beautiful piece of clothing she'd ever worn, even if it was definitely beyond her normal style. Alana wanted a mirror to see the full effect.

Fliss shook her head. "There are no mirrors in the castle, or still ponds, or anything with a reliable reflection. It just isn't safe."

"Have the Shades gotten in?"

"Once." Fliss dropped her gaze. "We lost my big sister that day."

Reflexively, Alana eyed the room. She wondered if the beautiful chamber had been the scene of the tragedy.

"I wouldn't worry," Fliss said lightly. "You look wonderful."

"Does it cover everything?"

"Do you mean your scars? Almost, but really, don't be concerned about them." Fliss sounded slightly envious. "They make you look like someone a dragon can respect."

Alana held out her arms, entertained by the trailing cuffs that were edged in silver bells. They gave a sweet tinkle whenever she moved—which would eventually annoy her, but not yet.

A knock sounded at the door. Alana expected another of the servants who had been coming and going with food, clothes, and toiletries. She had been distracted by their presence, though Fliss seemed to barely notice they were there. This time, however, it was Ronan who entered.

Fliss rose with an innocent expression. "I should see if the chamberlain needs anything." And then she left.

Ronan had changed clothes as well, and appeared every inch a prince in dark silks and velvet. The only embellishment was black embroidery along his cuffs and collar. The tiny stitches looked like ebony flames.

"Hello," he said, taking her in.

Alana smiled. "I like your sister. She's very bossy."

"Fliss was a young hellion when I saw her last."

"I don't think much has changed."

A silence followed in which they simply gazed at one another. Ronan seemed happy, and no wonder. He was back with his family and the role he'd been meant to fulfill. Now she could see everything he'd lost. A sweet pain, almost like nostalgia, filled her. Perhaps it was longing on his behalf. Perhaps it was regret, because it soon turned to heaviness.

The problem was that he couldn't have his old life back. When Fliss had been out instructing the servants, Alana had stowed the lamp under the floorboards beneath her bed. It was safe for now, but the curse that tied him to it was far from broken. She'd used two wishes. If she used the third, their bond would be over, and who knew what Ronan would be compelled to do.

"Why not tell your father and sister everything that's happened?" she asked. "Why are you pretending everything is fine?"

He closed his eyes. "I thought I would, as soon as I got my bearings. But an hour in this court, with these officers, has shown me what's really here."

"What do you mean?"

"Fliss is doing an amazing job running things, but most want to see her married. Father is no help. The officers are squabbling. Bright Wing is on the brink of collapse from within."

"And you think you can save it?"

Ronan gave his head a slight shake. "They think I can save it. It's my duty to try."

"But..."

"I can't leave Fliss without support." Ronan began to pace, moving to the window and back with the coiled grace of a leopard. "Besides, we came here because we were chasing Corby. We wanted to stop him, and ultimately the Shades. With Bright Wing, we have an army of dragons to help us do it. Maybe now we have a chance of success."

He had a good point, but there was a flaw. "How are you going to fight?"

His half-smile was amused. "With a sword. I'm under a vow to abandon my beast form until you agree to marry me."

Alana sat on a window seat, suddenly exhausted. "Is anyone actually going to believe that? I'm about as far as it gets from a princess. My foster parents think my mother was a forest fae, but I don't even know that for sure. My father is a complete mystery, but I'm certain he was no king."

He stopped in his tracks, regarding her. "They will believe us. My people love you for bringing me back. Give them a chance to love you for yourself."

Alana shook her head. That goodwill wouldn't last once they knew the truth. This was a bunch who didn't take chances, with no mirrors in the house and the patriarch in permanent dragon-mode.

Ronan approached the window seat, holding out his hands. "The truth is, Alana, if something happens to me, Bright Wing has the best chance of keeping you safe."

Alana reached for her knife hilt, only to grab a handful of silky folds. She shook them off with disgust. "How about *I* keep *you* safe?"

His eyes softened, and he folded her in his arms. Alana buried her face in his chest, searching for a sense of stability. Everyone here seemed adrift. The king in his vigil and the queen dead from grief. Fliss scrambling to keep things together. Ronan believing he could somehow defeat the monster who held him in chains. She wasn't much better, in this ridiculous dress and in the arms of a lover she could never keep, however this story ended.

"How did I end up here?" she murmured. "I wanted vengeance for Tina. Now I've got dragons and dark tyrants and a princess fending off her suitors!"

"My apologies," Ronan said, stroking her cheek with his thumb. "I've complicated your life."

"It's not a joke. I don't know what to do."

He tilted her face up to his. "You always make the right choice. You lead with your heart."

"What do you mean?"

"You confronted Henry today. He disappointed you, yet you saved him in the end. If you hadn't, we never would have discovered Corby's true nature."

"But that got us here, deep in enemy territory."

He stroked her hair. "With a dragon army at our backs. Trust what we've accomplished."

The next kiss lightly brushed her eyelids, then her nose and chin, and finally her mouth. He cherished her with each touch, letting her know how much he wanted her by his side. Alana melted beneath him, but she took as good as she got, drinking him in with a thirst she'd never known.

His fingers slid along her jaw, to the sensitive spot behind her ear. Alana shivered and angled her chin, giving him better access. His lips brushed her ear, then followed the slope of her shoulder to the neckline of her gown. The rush of his breath against her skin sent tingling along every nerve. She reached up, stroking his cheek while the silver bells on her sleeve tinkled faintly.

Ronan's fingers slid beneath the wide neckline of her gown to find her hardening nipple. His touch made her gasp, but he stopped the sound with a kiss.

"Hush," he murmured. "Dragons have excellent hearing, and I wouldn't trust Fliss not to listen at a keyhole."

But he had her body pulsing, each stroke of her breast sending a throb of heat to her belly. She arched into his hand, demanding more until he pushed the bodice aside and took her with his hot, wet mouth.

Her fingers searched his unfamiliar clothes, finding the silver buttons of his jacket. The velvet and fine stitching were sensuous to touch, the shirt beneath a light material that clung to his sculptured frame. Through the gauze of her skirts, she felt the swelling hardness of his body. She pulled open his collar to kiss the soft skin at the notch of his throat. His clothes smelled of sandalwood, clean and spicy and warmed by his growing heat. His chest was lightly dusted with hair that arrowed downward as his torso narrowed to lean hips. She glided her fingertips below his waistband and chuckled at his sudden, choking breath.

When she did it again, he batted her hands aside and deftly undid those buttons himself. His hard length filled her hands with a generosity that made her pulse quicken. Ronan advanced, forcing her to walk backward toward the bed. Alana moved carefully, the last rational part of her mind anxious about tripping on her gown. That was too slow for an impatient prince. Ronan lifted her by the waist, setting her on the edge of the bed and skimming his hands up her thighs to push aside the filmy cloud of her skirts.

By then, she was more than ready to take him, though his first thrust drew an indiscreet cry from her lips. His laugh was barely audible, but oh so male. Their lovemaking was slow, a thorough exploration of stolen pleasure that ended in a long, bruising kiss.

Afterward, Alana lay curled in Ronan's arms, her dress finally discarded in a drift upon the floor. She traced his features with her fingertips, marveling at his strong, boldly drawn features.

"Should I be honored, catching the fancy of a prince?" she teased.

He caught her hand, then tenderly placed a kiss in her palm. "I am the one who is honored. A title is mere words, Alana. Be the princess that you already are, and you will rule every heart."

❧ 14 ❧

"What do you mean, you don't dance?" Fliss asked as she stood in front of the great wardrobe that held all her dresses. She was the same height as Alana, and her clothes were a close enough fit to share. "Everyone can dance."

"I can dance in place while hitting somebody," Alana said, a touch sullenly. "It's a thing where I come from."

Fliss managed an eyeroll that would have been a credit to any human high-schooler. She then took down a gown before holding it up to Alana. "You'll just have to do your best. Wear something long enough that no one can see your feet."

"Why do I have to dance?" Alana backed away, regarding the pink confection with a frown.

"It's a ball. You and Ronan are the guests of honor. Deal with it. It's a thing where I come from." Fliss was picking up Alana's slang like an eager parrot. Giving up on the pink, the princess considered something yellow. "No, you'll look like a parsnip in that."

"Can't I visit the armory instead?" Maybe Alana could wish herself out of this?

"You can't have fun all the time." Ronan's sister gave a pout. "I'd rather be on a battlefield most days, but there's work to be done at the castle."

"You fight?" Alana asked in surprise.

"Give me a bow and I'll show you," Fliss grinned. "I've had just as many adventures as some of the generals strutting around these halls."

As Fliss had predicted, proper war councils had begun the day after their arrival. Alana attended but said little. She counted herself a warrior, but her fights had been against no more than a handful of opponents at a time. She knew nothing of armies, and less—if that were possible—about dragon armies. Keeping her mouth shut and her ears open seemed like the smart move.

She was rewarded by learning a lot, not just about attack vectors and ground maneuvers, but about how the captains regarded Ronan. He had been an unbeatable general until his disappearance. Now his return was hailed in almost mythical terms as a sign that the tides of war had turned. Even those jockeying for positions of power bowed to his leadership. Murmurs in the castle halls took on a note of hope.

There was only one holdout, in Alana's mind. "What do you make of Captain Jenowan?"

"That idiot?" Fliss curled her lip. "He fancies himself one of my suitors."

"Oh really?" That surprised Alana. Even she could see their personalities would never match. "I take it you aren't a fan?"

"He likes my title far more than he likes me. I suppose becoming heir to the throne of Bright Wing would suit him very well—or it would have. Now he's sulking because Ronan is back and spoiling all his plans."

"The entire Wheel is at stake," Alana said. "There's no room for drama."

"Teetering on the cusp of extinction doesn't deter fools from being fools." Fliss held up a blue dress covered in a net of seed pearls. "Now this one says Alana."

RONAN CLIMBED TO THE CRAG TO VISIT HIS FATHER, GRATEFUL for the chance to escape the clamor of the council and its opinions. It had been a fruitful session, but Ronan had much to catch up on from his absence. Covering even the highlights had made the meeting long. Now his mind was full of options, plans, and risks to manage. Each of the captains had been given tasks, and they had dispersed until it was time to reconvene for that evening's ball. That would be the highlight of his homecoming—for this one night, everyone would celebrate. Alana would glimpse what the fae world had been like before the coming of the Shades.

He opened the oak door, striding through onto the crag. The great dragon was back, lying in the same position as when Ronan had arrived home. The carpet he'd enchanted was now rolled up and propped against the side of the cliff.

"Father?" Ronan said quietly, wondering if the dragon was asleep.

But no. The orange eye swiveled in his direction. Ronan approached slowly and sank down in the shelter of his father's flank, just as he had as a boy. Back then, his father had been the stern embodiment of wisdom, of everything Ronan wanted to be. He'd been part of the Council of the Wheel and the right hand of the mighty Jorwarth, High King of the Faery Realm. Ronan remembered the lords of the council—kings, queens, princes, and wise bards—in their shining armor and jeweled robes. Back then, in those days of childhood, it seemed nothing could shake the deep roots of his world. But war had come, and so many deaths. Before his final battle, he had carried his mother's still form to her funeral pyre.

Now his father had retreated—whether from grief, exhaustion, or disappointment Ronan couldn't say. Dragons had no speech to share their thoughts.

For a long moment, they sat in silence, watching the flight of the patrols crisscrossing the plains.

"I know it's been a long, hard time for you, Father," Ronan said gently. "I'm sorry I've been gone."

The dragon gave a snort of steam. Ronan interpreted it as a signal to keep talking. "I've come to help in any way I can. So far, the captains seem solid. On the whole, though, Fliss has more common sense than most of them combined."

At that, the king turned his head.

"Of course I had her at the table. And Alana. The younger captains are too eager to please, and I need a range of opinions."

The dragon rumbled.

"I'm not the dragon I was when I left," Ronan replied. "I didn't leave of my own free will. I was angry, then despairing, and finally numb. I was forced to learn a great deal about humility and endurance."

His father went very still.

"And then I met Alana, who changed everything. If something happens to me, I need you and Fliss to look out for her. This isn't her world, and she'll need someone to show her the way."

His father gave no sign he'd heard, so Ronan pushed on. "Another thing. I could use your help with the officers. Like I said, there are some who are eager to do everything I say just because I'm telling them what to do. They want a strong leader who is visibly in charge."

And didn't abandon them like you did. His anger pushed him to say it, but his father had suffered and criticism would be cruel. Ronan would find a way to say what was in his heart when it wouldn't destroy the bridge he was trying to build.

"Unfortunately," Ronan continued, "there are others used to having their own way. They're all smiles now, but pulling them together will be a challenge. If you could demonstrate that you're behind me, that would go a long way."

The dragon pushed itself up to sit on its haunches, then rumbled. Ronan got to his feet, watching as the king slid from the ledge and into the air, spreading wings that seemed to span the horizon. He was gone again, retreated to the solitude of the sky. Ronan had asked for support, but had been left alone.

So this was what Fliss had endured all this time. No wonder she had wept in relief when he'd shown up. By rights, he should be able to take some of the load off her slim shoulders. Except— wasn't he simply an actor giving the illusion of a dragon prince?

But what other options were there? His chest ached with discontent and discouragement. Ronan could do nothing—like his father—or he could fight with what strength he had. There was no question which path made more sense, even if it seemed built upon quicksand.

He descended the stairs only to meet Jenowan on the way up. The young captain awarded him with a narrow-eyed glare as he bowed. "My prince."

"You were not at the war council," Ronan said. "I would have liked to see you there."

"Your Highness, I have regular duties to attend to."

"As does everyone else, yet they still came."

It was the verbal game of thrust and counter-thrust, polite but still cutting. Ronan held back, preferring to win by persuasion.

Jenowan inclined his head. "A thousand pardons, but my orders are from His Majesty, from before the time he took up his vigil."

"I am His Majesty's general and his son."

"Very good, my prince." Another bow. "I will deliver my report now, to His Majesty."

Ronan barely restrained the impulse to snarl. "My father is in the air. You're making the climb for nothing."

After a perfect and correct bow, Jenowan retreated the way he had come.

Taking a moment to cool his temper, Ronan started to follow. "Jenowan."

The captain turned.

Ronan regarded him from a few steps above. "Give me a chance to prove myself, and we will succeed. If we quarrel, we will fall to the enemy."

Jenowan's mouth thinned. "I've been here fighting all this time, Your Highness. I have been doing the necessary work."

Ronan bowed his head at the reproof. "You are required to obey orders. Do you understand?"

Jenowan gave a tight nod. "Very good, sir." Turning, he disappeared into the castle.

Ronan continued more slowly, his thoughts still turning over the captain's resistance. Punishment was the wrong answer this early in the game—a whipped horse never ran with all its heart. Sadly, coaxing him would be hard work, especially when the previous leadership had given up. Still, hard or not, it was the right thing to do.

Ronan sighed. Maps and tactics were always the smallest part of command. People took all the time and energy.

He saw signs of Fliss's handiwork well before he reached the ballroom. All the old decorations he remembered had been put up—festoons of ribbon, extra candles, and fragrant green boughs from the mountainside. As he passed the room where a buffet was set up, the scent of savory meats and warm bread tempted him to peek in. If there was less food overall because of the war, what they had was presented with style. As hostess of the ball, Fliss had done herself proud.

He'd no sooner thought of his sister than she bounced into view. "There you are," she cried, slipping her arm through his and steering him toward the main ballroom. "You need to show up on time. You're the guest of honor, the hero of the hour, and the great hope we've come to celebrate."

"I haven't done anything yet," he protested, but he understood why Fliss had organized the event despite the short notice. It was a symbol of the good old days. People needed evidence that Bright Wing's royal family was in charge again. More than that, they needed relief from the endless dark times.

They entered the enormous ball room with its polished parquet floor. Once, it had been filled with mirrors on every wall, but they had been taken down and replaced with potted trees hung with thousands of conjured points of light. "This is beautiful," he said to Fliss. "You've done an amazing job."

"You haven't seen the half of it," she whispered. "You wouldn't believe who I convinced to come."

That certainly piqued his curiosity. He let Fliss lead him through the crowd—again, not as many as he remembered from his youth—and stopped when they reached a knot of the older officers. A few stepped back, and he stared into the face of Laren of the Outward Isles.

"Well met, old friend." Holding a fist to his heart, Laren bowed.

"Too long." Ronan abandoned formality, thumping him on the shoulder. "You fought at our side from the day you left school. No need for fine manners now."

"Well said." Laren laughed, his sea-green eyes lighting up with pleasure. He was a water fae from the nobility, with long fair hair and gently pointed ears. His cousin, Harin, had looked much the same before he had become Blacktongue, corrupted by the Shades inside and out.

The water fae lifted his glass. "Tonight is for celebration. Tomorrow, we will discuss business."

"What business?" Ronan asked.

"Word reached us of your coming," Laren cast a glance at

Fliss, who no doubt had sent that message. "I've been sailing night and day with a mutual defense treaty from our council."

Another look between Laren and his sister, which brought a flush of pink rising up Fliss's cheeks. There was something going on there, and Ronan's big-brother instincts went on alert.

Still, he tried to focus on the task at hand. "Is this a new proposal? I thought there would have been a pact in place before now."

Embarrassment crossed Laren's face, but he quickly hid it. "It lapsed some years ago. Your arrival gave our side confidence to start anew."

Ronan said something neutral, but his thoughts swirled. Their treaty had lapsed, but now it was under negotiation again. His presence made a difference. He *had* to make his situation work. "Excellent news, then, and all the more reason to be merry tonight."

A fierce smile curled Laren's lips. "From ash returns the fire." He drained his glass.

Those were the words the fae resistance used, a clear signal Laren was thinking ahead. The phrase sent a hot tingle down Ronan's backbone, as if strengthening his resolve. "From ash returns the fire." If the water fae joined the dragons, half the fae would be united against the Shades. Who would be next to join?

Fliss snapped him out of his reverie by thrusting a glass of wine into his hand. "Mingle," she ordered. "You two boys can play politics later."

Ronan obeyed, moving from group to group—and then he saw Alana. She was like the personification of summer, all golden hair and a simple blue gown that showed off her lithe form. It was every prince's dream, he supposed, to find that one woman at a ball, the one who would make everything right. She would make sense of all the burdens that came as heir to a crown—the wars, the politicking, all that endless protocol. Alana was the one who would walk with him through fire and flame for the good of their people.

He wanted that dream. He wanted Alana.

"Are you enjoying yourself?" he asked.

"Your officers are incredibly attentive," she said with a faint smile. "You wouldn't believe some of the kind offers I've had in the last half hour."

Unfortunately, Ronan could. They were full-blooded dragons, after all. "Become used to having me as your constant chaperone."

"But what if I want to amuse myself?"

She was teasing him, but the pictures floating through his head made him want to incinerate something. He narrowed his eyes. "I need my soldiers fighting fit. You're not allowed to damage them. You're not allowed to make me want to crisp them, either."

Her lips quirked up in a mischievous half-smile that made her look like a naughty child. Heat flashed through him, bringing to mind the bedrooms just a few minutes away.

As if on cue, servants brought out a vast silver basin packed with ice and filled with bottles of the castle's best sparkling wine. Like every other reflective surface, the sides of the basin were draped in cloth to protect it from the Shimmer. They set it on its own pedestal, giving it a place of honor. At once, the servants began serving the pale, bubbling vintage.

"Three cheers for the Prince of Bright Wing!" cried Laren.

"Huzzah!" echoed the crowd with one voice. "Huzzah! Huzzah!"

Then the group of wood sprites on the balcony, with their fiddles and drums, started the music again. It was impossible not to move to the beat.

"Shall we dance?" Ronan asked Alana.

"I don't dance."

"Of course you do."

He guided her onto the floor, using the slightest touch of his power to relax her into the song. She had an athlete's awareness of her body and the natural grace of the fae. All she had to do was believe in her own sense of the music.

Eventually she did, and she was amazingly beautiful as she danced. Ronan's heart did a strange tumble as he turned her in his arms, feeling the pressure of her swaying body against his. By the time they slowed to a stop, he could barely remember his name.

They returned to the clumps of chatting guests as the next round of dancers took the floor. Evidently, Fliss had drunk a fair amount of the sparkling wine, given the tiny burst of flame she released whenever she hiccupped.

"How fortunate that I'm a water fae," Laren said, dutifully dousing an errant ember. Then he kissed her cheek as he removed the wineglass from her hand.

Ronan changed direction, steering Alana toward the food and out of Fliss's range. His sister deserved her fun, but this was Alana's first introduction to the court. It wouldn't do to scare her.

Ronan had almost reached the door when a newcomer arrived. He stopped dead in his tracks, gripping Alana's hand. The figure was neatly dressed, upright and strong, though his face was lined with care.

"*Father*," Ronan exclaimed, and the room grew still.

Ronan fell to one knee. Alana curtsied low beside him.

King Vass took a long step forward, then raised them both up. "I apologize for my late arrival to your welcome-home celebration."

Then he embraced Ronan hard. For an instant, Ronan allowed himself to be lost in the comfort of his father's arms. Tears stung the backs of his eyes, but he forced them down. Now was the time to be steady, and the strong heir his father wanted to see.

"You're back," Ronan said softly.

"As are you," his father said. "Your return has given me much-needed courage."

The king turned to Alana then, taking her hands. "Thank you

for being here, my dear. You've brought a fresh spark to this place."

Fliss gave an ear-splitting whistle, then shrugged when all eyes turned her way. "Music, play on! Let there be dancing! The celebration has truly begun!"

❧ 15 ❧

Alana swirled into another dance, and once again her feet knew what to do. She wasn't sure how or why—she hated dancing. And yet, she didn't. Not now. Not with Ronan. She was as light as down and dazed with happiness.

To her eyes, so was he. She wasn't certain what had taken place between Ronan and his father, but it had healed a serious breach. As if a curtain had been drawn back, lightness filled the air and everyone breathed easier.

So it seemed perfectly natural when her lips met Ronan's in a kiss, even though it took place on the dance floor and in full view of the entire company. They belonged to each other, and neither cared who saw it.

His lips were warm and soft and tasted of wine. Her fingers stroked the velvet of his fitted jacket, feeling the strength of his body beneath the fabric as he moved. She recalled the same warmth, the same sensation of living flesh, but skin to skin beneath the sheets. If she had her way, this celebration would return to the bedroom... and go on and on until the dawn broke over the mountaintops.

"I love you," he said, and everything fell away but the emotion in his eyes.

She went numb, as if disembodied from her physical self. No one had ever said that to her before, and her voice vanished as if she had never learned to speak. She kissed him again, trying to put everything she couldn't say into her touch.

The dancing grew frenzied, with stamping and spinning and wild leaps into the air. Everyone who could was dancing now, filling the ballroom floor. Alana was bumped and jostled, but she didn't care. Laughter rang throughout the castle.

Inevitably, someone knocked over the stand with the basin of ice. The wine had been drunk, so there were no bottles to smash, but chunks of ice skittered across the floor and made the dancers slip. Feet skating and arms waving, three people fell. But that was not the real disaster.

The basin rolled away with a hollow rumble until it clanged against the wall. By the time it stopped, it had lost the linen that covered its sides. The silver beneath gleamed, the high polish making a perfect mirror.

By the time Ronan grabbed a cloth to throw over it, it was too late. The air seemed to solidify before them, turning dark and glassy and shuddering like a pond when the earth trembled around it.

The Shimmer.

Ronan grabbed Alana's hand, pulling her away. Everyone else fell back as well, and the room whispered with the slide of drawn blades. Someone was shouting for more weapons—bows, arrows, spears, and whatever implements of magic that could be found.

All the fears of the dragons came to pass. Figures stepped through the Shimmer. At first, Alana couldn't tell who or what they were. The Shimmer's darkness clung to them like smoke that melted slowly away. A number of the invaders bolted from the ballroom and down the corridors. Several dragons gave chase, but most stayed where they could protect their king and his family.

Warriors ranged themselves around the Shimmer, weapons drawn and ready to pounce on any additional invaders—and there was more and worse to come. As the dark smoke peeled away, Alana's eyes fixed on the limp form of Captain Jenowan cradled in Hugo Martigen's arms.

"Martigen?" Alana said aloud. She'd suspected him of collusion with the investor—presumably a Shade—but this was far beyond writing checks to the dark side.

The older male dumped the officer onto the floor. By the boneless way Jenowan fell, Alana could tell he was dead. Someone cried out, and sick rage rose up the back of Alana's throat.

A terrible expression crossed Ronan's face—a mix of grief, guilt, and disappointment. A handful of uniformed men took steps forward, but Ronan held up a hand. "What is this, Martigen?"

"Your man was out patrolling alone," Martigen replied coolly into the stunned silence. "Or he was about to. As you can see, he hadn't changed to his dragon form."

Despite herself, Alana cast her gaze to the dead soldier. Jenowan appeared fully human, and only his jacket was unbuttoned. From what little she knew, a dragon took ages to shift due to the complexity of the transformation, not to mention the size difference.

"One might ask," Martigen continued, stepping over the corpse to approach Ronan, "why he was by himself. Friends never let friends shift alone. It's a vulnerable moment—or hours, if one is a dragon."

"Do you have a point?" Ronan demanded.

"Indeed I do. The spies who caught your man learned his fellow officers were celebrating the return of their prince. Everyone was to attend, leaving the mountain unguarded. He apparently disapproved of such frivolity, so he planned to mount a patrol on his own. After all, if something went wrong, it would be *hours* before a dragon could come and burn the villains to ash!"

Sounds of battle broke from the corridors, and in one sinking moment, Alana knew the ball had been a mistake. Corby—wearing his normal face now—appeared from behind Hugo.

"No one invited us," the bookseller said, sarcasm thick in his tone. "Bad luck!"

Chaos broke loose in the ballroom. Alana reached beneath her skirts, drawing the blade she'd strapped to her thigh. Ronan smashed Corby in the jaw, knocking him down, but Fliss's scream stopped everyone in the immediate area cold.

Martigen had her pinned, a blade at her throat. The position was awkward, with Martigen standing behind her, but it was effective enough that Laren had frozen a few feet away, sword in hand but afraid to risk the princess's life.

"Get off me," Fliss snarled, clawing at Hugo's fingers, "or I will eat you!"

Martigen gave a harsh laugh. "I'd have your head off before you'd sprouted a single scale."

"Endanger my sister and I'll kill you myself," Ronan bellowed.

Alana stood to one side, the knife hidden in her skirts. As Corby picked himself up, his gaze turned her way. An unpleasant smile curved his bleeding lips. "So this is where you got to. You and I have a debt to settle. Or should I say you have an exit interview to complete?"

Despite herself, Alana gulped.

King Vass appeared at her side, a battle ax in one hand. "Leave Lady Alana in peace." His voice was firm, but he strained like a dog on a leash, desperate to attack but afraid for his daughter.

"*Lady* Alana?" Corby laughed. "Seriously?"

"What do you want, crow?" the king roared—there was no other word for it. Alana felt the sound through her shoes.

"Stay where you are," Corby shouted back.

"How dare you enter my castle?" Vass bellowed, a vein in his forehead ticking his rage.

Corby all but hopped from foot to foot, excitement bright in his eyes. "This should only take a moment, and we'll be on our way."

"What will?" Ronan started forward, but Hugo did something that made Fliss whimper. Ronan stopped, eyes blazing.

Alana's stomach was a ball of ice. She inched slowly to the left, studying the position of each speaker in relation to her blade. Martigen was also watchful, taking care to keep Fliss between himself and the dragons. True, they were loud and had big swords, but it never paid to forget about the foot soldiers. Alana saw her chance, slipping up from behind and driving her blade into his ribs. He half-turned toward her, mouth opened in silent horror, the shock on his face absolute.

"Gotcha," Alana murmured.

Fliss twisted free, making way for Laren to thrust his sword through her captor's heart. The dragon princess was safe.

A moment later, more Shades oozed through the portal, this time attacking the ballroom directly. As if a switch had flipped, the room exploded into violent motion. King Vass, with Ronan at his side, were in the thick of it, shredding the invaders. Alana spun, ready to take out Corby next. Around her, the sounds of battle crashed and shrieked as dragons and Shades tore the castle apart. None of it touched her. Alana's breathing was calm, her heart steady. Battle was where she was at her best.

"Take that one," Corby shouted, pointing her way. "Bring her to me so I can settle our score."

A handful of Shades turned her way. These weren't the short, bearded creatures she'd met before. These were tall, whip-thin, and wearing hoods that covered their faces. She crouched, calculating which to take first, and which one was likely to end her life. With a flick of her gaze, she mapped where every one of her allies stood. They were all fighting enemies of their own. Corby had her isolated.

As one, the Shades surged. Alana danced—her kind of dancing now—evading and thrusting, using every one of Henry's tricks for fighting multiple opponents. One went down, then two. Her feet caught in her long skirts, but she kicked them free. She'd already lost her flimsy shoes. Whirling to swipe at her third attacker, she unexpectedly went down, losing her knife. She struggled to get up, but her limbs were trapped. It was only when she tried to roll over that she realized she was tangled in a net.

Alana struggled, wriggling her fingers through the mesh to reach her knife, but the trap snugged tighter. She cursed, realizing it was enchanted. Every time she moved, it shrank.

Someone grabbed her feet, then began dragging her Corby's way.

"Alana," Ronan cried, pushing through the mob.

She twisted and squirmed, but had to give up when the net threatened to choke her. Alana could just see Ronan's face. She could see Corby's, too, and read the delight there. She'd shot him, and now he'd get his vengeance. Okay, so he was happy about that —but with Ronan crashing toward him, why wasn't he afraid?

The answer came immediately. A Shade slipped into the room carrying something bright. *The lamp!* A cry of rage and horror escaped Alana. There it was, the ballroom's candlelight softly brushing its golden sides. She'd hidden it so well not even the castle's servants had found it, yet Corby's men—no doubt aided by his ability to sniff out magical objects—had located it within minutes.

Ronan reached the front of the milling crowd, ready to rescue Alana. Corby was only a dozen steps away, taking the lamp from his minion. The moment he touched the dragon-embossed sides, Ronan turned to stone, all color draining from his cheeks.

With both hands, Corby held up his prize so that all could see. There was chaos and fighting all around, but that didn't deter him. He had the audience he wanted—Ronan, King Vass, and a handful of officers. Next to them, Laren held Fliss in his arms.

"Behold," Corby shouted. His smile split into a gloating grin that made Alana writhe with fury. "Here is the truth about your reclaimed prince. He is not worthy to call himself heir to your crown. He was conquered long ago—bound to the confines of this lamp—which is where he shall return!"

An enraged bellow shook the castle, followed by cries of disbelief. Confusion flew through the room like wildfire, causing one fight after another to break apart. From her place on the floor, Alana could see many of the invaders lying dead. Even without wings or fire, the dragons had been winning. Now the remaining Shades used Corby's distraction to make their retreat. The fight had been an effective cover for their real objective—theft—and now they were done.

Alana didn't have much time to escape. She found Ronan's gaze and silently pleaded for aid, but there was only devastation in his eyes. He couldn't help her. Now that someone else had possession of the lamp, she was no longer his master.

A heartbeat later, he dissolved into mist, swirling into the spout of the lamp. One by one, the dragons fell still, their expressions stunned by what they witnessed. King Vass surged forward, Fliss on his heels with her eyes a murderous gold.

But Corby was too quick. With a cackle, he tucked the lamp under his arm and snatched up the net that bound Alana tight. Quick as a bird, he hopped through the Shimmer, dragging her behind him. The last she saw of the Wheel was Fliss and the king, their faces white with agony.

ALANA WOKE SLOWLY, HER MIND GROPING THROUGH FOG. Cold, dank air clung to her like sticky fingers. When she cracked her eyes open, she could see little but a murky pool of light. Where was she?

After a few tries, she convinced her hand to move and explore. The floor was concrete, but she was lying on a vinyl mat that smelled of sweat and mildew. A wave of revulsion swept through her, and she pushed herself upright. Her head swam, but she realized the net that had bound her was gone. That was positive, at least.

She wasn't alone. Barleycorn sat on a bench with his back to the wall, regarding her as if she were an interesting experiment. "How do you feel?"

Alana drew her knees up, curling into herself for warmth. She was still wearing the flimsy gown, torn and filthy from the fight. "How do you think?" she shot back.

"Are you injured?"

That was a good question, so she checked herself. "No, but something knocked me out."

"That was a spell. Nasty, but there should be no lasting effects."

She glanced around the room, realizing she knew the place. "This is one of the cells beneath the arena." Every so often, a fae prisoner took part in the fights as a means to shorten their sentence.

"Correct."

Her gaze flew to Barleycorn as the reality of her situation hit home. She was tingling from head to foot, her pulse pounding with shock. The fog that had cushioned her thoughts ripped away, and she recalled everything—the battle, her capture, and the wild despair in Ronan's eyes. "Why am I here?"

He gave a slow nod, as if he'd expected the question. "There was a compromise. Corby simply wanted you dead, publicly and with as much indignity as possible. Martigen, on the other hand, wanted the money a spectacular grudge match would bring."

"Martigen is dead."

"I'm referring to Tyrell."

She sucked in a breath. So Tyrell had thrown her to the wolves as well. She had crap luck in bosses. "I'm to fight?"

"Tomorrow night. You against the Slash. As I said, a grudge match." He paused, actually appearing uncomfortable. "To the final blood."

She swore long and hard. The two cats had mauled her after Tina was down. Her muscles tensed, bracing against remembered pain. "So Corby gets his way, too."

Barleycorn's expression remained carefully controlled. "Why didn't you tell me about the lamp?"

"Why would I?" She glared. "I have no reason to trust you."

"I found you employment."

"With the guy who is planning my public execution."

"Fair enough. Any work experience can be unpleasant, but retail is often the worst." Barleycorn crossed his legs. "Do you even understand the nature of the lamp?"

"I know Ronan."

"Not the same thing. How many wishes have you used?"

"Two."

For the first time since she'd met him, Barleycorn looked worried. "You'll find it difficult to resist the third."

"I'm not Ronan's master anymore. Corby took the lamp."

"You may have no power over the genie's actions in general, but you can still claim that third wish. In fact, the magic of the lamp will do its best to tempt you."

"But don't give in," Alana said. "I know the drill."

"If you do, I guarantee you'll sell your soul to Blacktongue to get a fourth wish, or a fifth."

"Blacktongue?" She remembered the hideous face in the mirror.

"Who do you think made the lamp and trapped Ronan inside?"

Alana stared at Barleycorn. "What are you saying?"

"Three wishes is never enough. That's how it works. That's how he bends men like Martigen and Corby to his will. They may not have had possession of the lamp, but they will have faced similar temptations."

"But Harin's a water fae, not a Shade."

"As with Corby, there's not much fae in him now. Eventually, the Shades' corruption takes a toll."

That ghastly face drifted through her mind. "Why do they want the lamp? Can't Harin grant his own wishes?"

"Perhaps, but Ronan has a dragon's strength. Harin can harness that energy. Also, the lamp appears innocent, and turns up in places Harin could never go. He catches far more victims that way."

"Ronan said the lamp was a weapon." Now she understood.

"Did he?" Barleycorn raised a brow. "Few genii have the strength to say anything about their prison."

"But..." She hugged herself, her mind skating as if it had lost traction. "I never thought Ronan would hurt me!"

Barleycorn shook his head. "He's bound to encourage you to make wishes, whether he wants to or not."

"He did at first." She licked her lips, realizing she was parched. "Then not so much. Not after we grew... close."

Barleycorn's brows had gathered into a frown. "It sounds as if he tried to spare you. Take comfort in that."

She heard the "but" in his words, and waited.

Barleycorn made a slicing gesture with his hand. "You can't trust him, and you can't trust yourself. If you ever were incorruptible, you aren't now. Do not make any more wishes!"

You can't trust him. The words were acid in her mind. "Why do you care? What's your involvement in this?"

"I don't fancy being ruled by Shades. I put you in that bookstore to keep an eye on Corby."

"You *knew* he was up to something?"

"I knew Blacktongue had agents searching for the lamp. And I suspected Corby's collectibles business was engaged in an effort to find it again."

Alana's hurt was giving way to outrage. "So you stuck me in the middle of the war zone?"

"Certainly. You were one of the few people who could look

after yourself if something went awry. Plus, I thought you would be grateful enough to tell me what you observed."

"You assumed too much."

His mouth twisted into a wry smile. "Apparently. I knew I'd made a mistake the moment I saw you on a flying carpet. You fell in love with him. That wasn't part of my plan."

Alana looked away. That wasn't a topic for discussion, not with this man. "Why did you come here?"

They were both silent until Barleycorn cleared his throat. "The danger of the third wish. You needed to know. There isn't much I can do now that Corby is playing lord of the manor, but I could buy my way in here and tell you that much."

Alana supposed she should be grateful, but she was beyond emotion right then. "You bribed your way in?"

"Like I said, I'd rather not be ruled by Shades."

She slumped, rubbing her face with her hands. Would things be better if she'd told Barleycorn about the lamp—or Tyrell—the day he'd come into the store? Regrets were useless now, and she wouldn't trade the last few days with Ronan for anything. For that moment, they had been together and free.

"Thank you for telling me," she finally said.

"I owed you that much." Once he rose, he rapped to get out.

The lock rattled, and someone Alana couldn't see opened the door. A guard, she supposed.

Barleycorn turned. "I'll see to it that you get proper food and clothes."

She got to her feet, every muscle stiff from lying on the floor. She met his blue-gold gaze, managing somehow not to flinch. "I'm going to die, aren't I?"

His outward expression didn't change, but there was a hint of challenge in his eyes. "Probably."

❧ 16 ❧

"I don't know, girl," Tina said, holding up the costume that had just been delivered to their cramped dressing room. "Do pink rhinestones say I'm a bad-assed fae who's going to stomp on your face?"

"Everyone knows you will stomp wherever you please." Alana unfolded her own costume, which was identical but in blue. "Not even footie pajamas will change that."

Tina held the bodysuit up, swiveling this way and that in front of the mirror. How she could see her image past the clutter of nail polish, glitter dust, and hair products was a mystery to Alana. "I know. We're going all the way to the top, you and me. No one is going to change that."

"That's 'cause you trash talk the best."

"I scare them, don't I?" Tina grinned. "But we back up every word with pure lightning, baby. Those kittens are going down."

There was no reason to doubt it. This fight with the Slash would be tough, but everything was in their favor, down to the grandmas betting their bingo money. They were on top.

Still, there was a questioning note in Tina's voice. "What is it?" Alana asked. "What's wrong?"

Tina tossed the costume aside. It was for publicity photos, not for the *fighting circle, where they'd be wearing proper leathers. "Once we go all the way, win the title, drink the champagne, then what?"*

"What do you mean?"

"We're not interesting anymore."

"Huh?" Alana folded her arms. Things were never good when Tina got philosophical.

"You and me, right now, we're doing our best to topple the champions. Once we've done that, we become the old guard some up-and-comers have to beat. The crowd, they love the shiny new young'uns. That's why they want us now." Tina slumped into her chair. That was as long a speech as she ever made.

Alana sat, then scooted her own chair to Tina's side. She put a hand on her friend's knee. "We're not washed up yet, y'know."

Tina laughed, a throaty, boisterous sound. "No, girl, not yet. But I want that champion's bonus, so I can get the hell out. Maybe I'll open a nice nail salon—make people pretty instead of messing them up for a living."

THE SOUND OF A KEY IN THE CELL DOOR JERKED ALANA OUT OF the past. She hadn't had a visitor since Barleycorn's appearance the day before. She almost welcomed the interruption, even though there was no one she wanted to see.

"I'm sorry to disturb you," Tyrell Martigen said. Although he was dressed in one of his costly suits, he looked haggard with fatigue.

She almost felt sorry for him until she recalled he was making money off her death. "Memories aren't always the best company. What can I do for you?"

He shifted, looking everywhere until he finally brought his gaze to her. His hands bunched into fists. "I want to know how my father died."

"Holding a knife to the throat of a princess." There was no reason to soften the truth.

The skin around his eyes tightened. "He wasn't always like that."

Alana leaned her head against the wall. "I suppose not. None of us start out as killers."

"Blacktongue promised things that made my father into someone I don't—didn't—recognize."

"Then maybe your father died a long time ago."

For a moment, she thought Tyrell was about to cry.

"Is Blacktongue the investor?" she asked.

He jerked his head up, eyes wide. "How do you know about Blacktongue?"

She shrugged. "Just curious."

He didn't answer. She supposed that was as good as a yes.

"There's nothing more to say." Tyrell blew out an exasperated breath.

She had a crazy impulse to laugh. "Maybe not."

He stuffed his hands in his pockets. "Any last requests?"

"Just one."

His shoulders went tight, but he nodded.

"I want the page from the betting book for the night Tina died."

"No."

She hadn't expected him to agree, but the refusal still rankled. "Did you order Tina's death to get a bigger payout on the fight?"

He stared up at the ceiling, as if he stored his patience there. "I make money on fighting, but it's the industry standard. My odds compilers balance the books, but that's all."

"You place your own bets. I saw the slips on your coffee table, remember?"

"Those weren't in my name."

"They were with your pocket change and lottery tickets. Whoever placed those bets, you were personally interested in whether they won. That says all anyone needs to know." She paused just long enough for him to glower. "So did you do it?"

He turned and pounded on the door, just as Barleycorn had done.

"I hope you didn't come in search of forgiveness." Alana crossed her legs. "Blacktongue corrupted your father. What's your excuse?"

The door opened. He paused, turning hard eyes her way. "Would it help to know it was me?"

"I swore on her grave I would find out." Alana sat forward, elbows on her knees. "I don't like unfinished business."

His jaw tightened, and she read the momentary panic in his eyes. She tried to savor it, since it was as close as she'd get to justice.

Tyrell left without another word.

Hours passed. Food came. She braided her hair in tight multiple rows, pinning it close to ensure it couldn't be used as a handhold during the fight. Then her gear arrived. With a pang, she realized Henry must have kept it. It was cleaned and repaired, every stitch and buckle in top shape.

It was a kindness, but it wouldn't be enough to save her. She'd faced these two fighters before. They were good, better than good, with a tiger's instinct for blood. In an honest fight, she could take one of the pair. With Tina, they could have defeated both, but Tina wasn't around anymore.

Alana pulled on her boots, checking every fastening to make sure they were secure. Habit, training, discipline—these were her friends now. She couldn't afford a mistake if she wanted to survive more than a minute.

The duo had crushed her before without breaking a sweat. In a fight to the last blood, when she was marked for a spectacular and public death, she didn't have a prayer. Even if she won—well, Corby and Tyrell would never let it happen.

Unless she used the third wish. Barleycorn had told her absolutely not to, but would Ronan really harm her that way?

Alana stood, shaking out her limbs to ensure her body armor

sat right, but then sank down again and put her head in her hands. If Ronan *could* have saved her, he would have done it when Corby had her in the net. Ronan's heart might be hers, but he was otherwise trapped.

But he still owed her one wish—and she could call on it. It had to be available despite the change in ownership, or Barleycorn wouldn't have warned her against using it. She could wish herself free, get vengeance for Tina, get the lamp from Corby, and fly back to the Wheel with Ronan.

Do it. Do it. DO IT!

Alana ground her eyes with the heels of her hands. "But it makes no sense," she murmured. Running that way was building on sand. The Shades would be after them forever. They took Ronan once; they could do it again.

She pulled her hands away. Tears slid down her cheeks, leaving salt on her lips. Pain flowered inside her, shredding her with might-have-beens. What good were future plans if she was dead by sunrise? How could she help Ronan then? Alana sobbed once, then clamped a hand over her mouth. The guards couldn't, *wouldn't*, hear her cry. She still had some pride left.

Maybe she could phrase the wish carefully, building in language to cover every loophole? She was no lawyer, but she'd always been clever. Surely she was good enough for this!

Yes, do it. DO IT!

Yet, Barleycorn had said using the third wish put her into Blacktongue's corrupting power. That was what had happened to Hugo Martigen and Corby. Would she end up like them? She'd wanted to be a bodyguard, offering protection for a living. Would the Shades make her an assassin instead? Twist the anger and sadness in her heart to something deadly?

It doesn't matter. Do it anyway. DO IT!

"Get lost," she muttered to the voice in her head. "You're the wish talking, and it's not gonna happen."

Wiping her face dry, Alana stood, checking her armor more

thoroughly this time. She was a fighter, and that meant trusting her own sweat, blood, and brutal honesty. There was no wishing in the circle, just doing.

Maybe—probably—this was her last fight. She'd go out on her own terms.

Alana straightened her spine, lifted her chin, then pounded on the door, summoning the guard.

By the time he opened it, she was focused on one thing only. "I'm ready."

The guards took no chances, chaining her hands and feet before letting her out of the cell. That, she supposed, was the price for being at the top of her game. When they led Alana down the passageway to the arena, she was only vaguely aware of the clamor of the crowd. She'd heard it so often it was part of the landscape, like the surf or wind in the trees.

Her gaze searched ahead until she found Henry in his customary spot. Although the circle didn't technically have corners, there was still a place for each fighter to retreat, with gear and people to support them. Despite everything, it felt right to have Henry in hers.

"You're here," she said when they were close enough to speak.

"Of course I am," he said gruffly, then eyed the shackles. "Get those off her, fools!"

She glanced around as the guards fiddled with keys. The cats hadn't arrived yet, so she squinted to see past the overhead spotlights into the stands.

There were boxes for the guests of honor, and she wasn't surprised to see Tyrell Martigen in the left-hand seat. On the far right was Corby, his chair hitched forward so his short, squat form could see over the balcony. He wouldn't want to miss a moment of her humiliating end. Alana's skin crept, but she forced herself to keep scanning the crowd. She recognized many of the faces and searched each one, wondering which were involved in the cabal to serve Blacktongue, aka the investor. Her instincts said more than a few, and certainly the ones in the expensive seats.

Once her limbs were free again, Henry rubbed his hands, clearly nervous. Then he helped her strap on her weapons under the watchful gazes of the guards.

"Okay, look," Henry said. "I've done some asking around. Toku had a shoulder injury a week ago. Go for the left side if you can. It's not been healing as fast as it should."

He went on, the flood of advice soothing and familiar. It was part of the routine Alana needed to calm down before the bell, and Henry knew it. He kept at it until a change in the crowd's murmur made him stop.

The Slash were coming out now, silk robes over their furred bodies. Fear instantly jolted Alana, reminding her how those claws and fangs had ripped at her flesh. Of how she'd been left, bad enough that they'd thought her dead. Her lungs froze, leaving her to sip for air until she grappled her panic and shoved it down. She already knew everything her fear had to tell her. She didn't need the warning.

She looked for Toku, who was bigger and had darker stripes than his brother. Sure enough, he was guarding his left side. Then she studied Riki, the small, quick one. He wasn't as crafty as he liked to think. There might be a chance to trip him up.

The emcee was in the circle now, doing his spiel. Alana started to fidget, missing what he said that made everyone go quiet. The entire arena turned to the guest of honor's seat. A figure emerged onto the balcony where Tyrell and Corby sat. Two of the Shades stood with him like ominous shadows. Beside her, Henry sucked in a breath.

"Who is that?" Alana asked under her breath, but she already knew the answer.

"Harin Blacktongue. Barleycorn said he would show himself tonight."

Ronan had described golden armor to her, but now Blacktongue was more simply dressed—if *simply* meant a hooded cloak and a creepy, full-face mask. She didn't blame him for hiding that ugly visage.

"Why is he here?"

Henry's look was hard to read. "You're a celebrity after giving Corby and Martigen a hard time."

Then she understood. Blacktongue intended to be public and present when she went down. That way, the rank and file got the point: disobedient equals dead. Like any good future conqueror, he was laying the groundwork for absolute rule—and the fact that Blacktongue was here surely meant invasion wasn't far off. How many times had he visited, threatening and bewitching fae like Corby and Hugo Martigen?

She wasn't the only one asking questions. The whispering around the room was getting louder. Even those who didn't seem to know about Blacktongue were looking anxious now. The emcee called for silence, so the fight could begin. As he left the circle, she glanced up to see Corby kneeling before Blacktongue and reluctantly handing over the lamp. It was plain he didn't want to do it, and equally plain he had no choice. Blacktongue waved a gloved hand, and Corby placed the lamp on the balcony rail. Was that so Alana could gaze on everything she'd lost?

Do it. Do it. DO IT!

Ronan stood at the back of the box, so still he might have been made of wax. Even so, his gaze was fixed her way. No doubt he would be forced to watch as she fought for her life. Slowly, a bit at a time, her heart broke in two. Unconsciously, her hand crept to press beside her breastbone and feel each aching beat.

One wish, and they could both be free to go.

Do it. DO IT!

Despair seized her. She turned and threw her arms around Henry, needing someone, anyone, to hold her. "Thank you for everything you've been to me."

He hugged her back. "Knock 'em dead. I know you will."

The bell rang.

Alana was out of time. No room to make decisions. No last chance to take the easy road. She was there to fight.

A sense of rightness stilled the yammering of the wish. She'd probably never know for sure if the cats had been part of the plot against her and Tina, or if that had been all Tyrell. Either way, they'd done far more damage than necessary to win. Now Alana would deliver a lesson: *Don't touch people I love.*

The Slash advanced. The two cats spread out, their bare feet silent on the circle's sandy floor. Henry gave Alana a final pat on the shoulder. Now that the fight had started, her nerves settled into a steady, alert hum. She strolled into the circle, keeping a casual air but making sure she could see both opponents. When they struck, she would need all the warning she could get.

Her hands flexed, but she didn't draw a weapon. No need to commit before it was time, and there was strategy in waiting. She would choose to match the nature of their attack.

Toku moved first, darting in with a slash of his claws. Alana kicked, knocking him back. Cats tired quickly, but it was game over if they got close enough to force their prey to the ground. Those hind claws could rip open soft tissue in seconds.

Toku tried again. This time, her heel landed squarely on his bad shoulder. He hissed, showing long eyeteeth.

A flick of his gaze made Alana give a sudden backward kick, catching Riki in the throat. Toku's tell had saved her from a sneak attack. She turned, repositioning while Riki coughed and spat.

The audience cheered, but she paid it no attention. The change of ground put her opposite the balcony where Ronan watched, as still and silent as before. Yet, even at this distance, she could see the sorrow and fury in his eyes.

Alana paid for her distraction. Toku tackled her from the side, knocking her to the ground. Alana took the brunt of the fall on her hip, then tried to roll away. He grabbed for her, finding the seams in her armor and digging his claws in to find flesh. Alana ripped away, scrambling to her feet with her ribs on fire.

She was barely upright when Riki pounced, jaws closing over her shoulder. Alana elbowed him before he could get a solid bite, then slammed the side of his jaw so hard he spun in place. Grabbing his arm, she twisted it until the pressure forced the joint the wrong way. She held that in place while she flicked the knife from her wrist sheath. "Start begging," she murmured in Riki's tufted ear.

"Alana!" cried a strangled voice from above.

Reflexively, she ducked, the knife Toku had thrown sinking into his brother instead. A collective gasp went through the room as Riki collapsed to his knees, the knife sticking from his side. Judging by the angle, it wasn't a lethal wound, but it must hurt. Toku gave a savage cry, his green eyes blazing, but he was the one to blame. That was the second mistake he'd made.

She'd been saved by someone's cry. Surely it had been Ronan's voice, but that wasn't possible, was it? Could he defy Blacktongue's magic to save her life?

He could, if you used the third wish.

Toku unwrapped a long chain from his waist. On the end was a flat disc of metal shaped like a starburst of sharpened points. He began spinning it like a lasso, working the chain with his short fingers. The blade sang through the air, sending chills over Alana's whole frame. She backed away, eyes fixed on the flashing metal. The fighting circle was large with plenty of room to move, but there was never enough space to run from something like this.

The audience had gone silent, so the only sound was the hum of the blade and Riki's moans. The smaller cat lay curled on the floor, cradling his wound. By the rules of the game, he couldn't leave the circle until the fight was done. That wouldn't happen until someone was dead.

Toku swung low, sending the blade snaking along the floor. Alana leaped over it, watching and listening for any change in tempo that could trick her into jumping too late. The next spin was higher, so she ducked. Then it looped, and she flipped, barely escaping the razor-sharp edge. She'd fought this weapon before, but never when it was in the hands of someone this good. Toku had been practicing, or else had magic on his side.

And then it was a running game, with the blade whipping after Alana like a fury. She leaped and scampered and spiraled like a gymnast, frantic to stay a split second ahead. But she soon began to tire. She'd have to end this if she meant to survive.

Bit by bit, Alana closed the distance between her and Toku until she was inside the reach of the flashing disc. With a sudden lunge, she grabbed the chain and hauled him forward. The disc flailed wildly, narrowly missing Toku's head. Caught off guard, he stumbled, and she used the momentum to wrap the chain around his neck and pull.

He fell to his knees, Alana behind him. Her breath was sawing in and out, so she barely heard the swell of the crowd's cheer. She glanced up to see Ronan right behind Corby, his face shining with perspiration. In his own way, he was fighting just as hard as she was. Then his eyes went wide.

Something clubbed her on the back of the head. The chain flew out of her hands, and Toku burst forward just as she fell on her face. Pain flared everywhere when that something hit again, and she realized Riki was up and stomping on her spine. And then Toku was on his feet as well, and she heard the scrape of a blade against leather. The fight was all but over, and she'd lost.

There was one last chance to wish before that blade came down. She gazed up into Ronan's agonized face. The third wish would break any bond she had with him, but she would lose him anyhow. Alana didn't want to die—but she sure as hell didn't want to live as Blacktongue's slave, either. No, even if her fight was over, the dragons weren't done. She could still help Ronan, even if it meant her death.

With a last desperate burst of strength, she pushed herself up. "Ronan, Prince of Bright Wing, I wish you free of the lamp forever!"

Startled, Toku hesitated, his blade in the air. Alana punched him, and he went down. Riki backed away, one hand gripping his side and the other pointing to the balcony. The real show was up there now.

Ronan had snatched up the lamp, which glowed as if it were molten. Corby was desperately reaching for it, but Ronan held it high above his head. Blacktongue sprang from his seat, the black cape billowing with the motion. With the mask, it was impossible to read his expression, but the Shades had stepped closer to him like cowering dogs. Blacktongue gestured with his hands, presumably to summon the Shimmer, but nothing happened. Maybe there was already too much magic at work.

Alana began laughing out loud as one of the Shades began beating the wall with its fists. Something was about to happen, and it wasn't going to be pretty. The dragons that decorated the side of the lamp were lifting off and floating in the air, swirling and merging and binding themselves into one huge beast. It was a spectacular dance of light and form that stretched up and up like taffy, then folded down to wrap around Ronan in a blaze of light. The lamp exploded, showering minuscule shreds of metal over the audience below.

Alana watched open-mouthed, getting to her feet without knowing she was doing it. A wild glee filled her and she thrust her fists in the air, letting out a mighty whoop. That lamp was *over*.

And then the railing of the balcony burst, scattering chairs and plaster and chunks of wood. People ran screaming, or else hung on where they could. Wings the color of clouds unfurled, filling the ceiling and muting the light. A howl rose from the crowd, triumph and terror in one unholy mix. Flames licked through the air, casting everything in shades of red.

Dragons might normally take hours to shift, but not when they were reverting from genie form.

The wings snapped closed, and Alana could see Ronan's dragon. Like his father, he was enormous, but he was a lighter shade, more mist than storm, the scales iridescent as pearl. She stared, awestruck and aghast. It was strange to see this other side of him, but it also felt exactly right. Her wish had done this—*she* had set him free—and he was beautiful and powerful and true. *This* was the prince destined to save his world. Tears spilled from her eyes, washing away the sweat and blood of the fight.

Corby was clinging to the remains of the balcony rail, screaming curses as he struggled not to fall. Steam huffed from the dragon's nostrils as his head swiveled toward Corby, the long neck graceful as a cobra. Then the huge jaws opened, displaying a double row of dagger teeth. Alana had just enough time to wonder what would happen next—and then Corby was no more.

Ronan swerved toward Tyrell next, but he leaped, choosing the thirty-foot drop from the balcony instead of the dragon's jaws. Alana squeezed her eyes shut.

But then she had to keep looking, because Blacktongue finally had the Shimmer open. His servants burst through, desperate for safety, leaving only Ronan and his nemesis. Alana knew, through the haze of her astonishment, that time and fate had circled back to where everything had begun. Now it was time for the Prince of Bright Wing's revenge.

But Ronan did the one thing she didn't expect. He turned his back on Blacktongue and dropped from the balcony with one lazy flap of wings—aiming directly for her.

Alana had forgotten the Slash or anyone else standing nearby, but now she was aware of them running for their lives. The entire arena was in chaos, with chairs crashing as panicked audience members climbed over each other in a rush for the doors. But she stood her ground, alone in the fighting circle and gazing up.

Her heart pounded, expectation crackling in her veins. The fact he'd chosen to find her first could only mean one thing. The lamp no longer bound them, but they still belonged together. She was no longer his keeper, but his partner, and they would fight side by side.

The place was too small for the dragon to land. All she could see was his underbelly, the palest gray edged with those pearlescent scales. But then he hovered, wings fanning the air, and she saw the thick forelegs ending in talons as long as scythes. He picked her up as delicately as a kitten. She was glad of her armor, but she had nothing to fear—although the sudden upward swoosh nearly left her stomach behind. He tucked her close and turned, launching back toward the Shimmer.

Blacktongue waited on what was left of the balcony. As they drew near, Alana got a closer look at him. He was tall and stooped, his wasted frame hidden by the cloak. The hood had slipped back to reveal long wisps of greenish hair and a lot of putrid scalp. All the same, he quickly moved to stand in front of the Shimmer. Clearly, he meant to block Ronan's path.

"Do you think to escape me, Prince of Bright Wing?" Blacktongue demanded, his deep, clear voice as sonorous as music. "Do you think our dance is done?"

Alana felt Ronan's sides heave as he inhaled, then he released a torrent of flame right at Blacktongue. The blast was precise and intense. Alana turned her face away, the scorching air washing over her. The smell of charcoal filled the underground arena.

She had to get away from that heat. Her fingers closed around the edges of Ronan's scales and she pulled herself up, finding plenty of footholds to scramble her way to the base of his expansive serpentine neck. It took only seconds. Wedging herself between two of the bony plates that ridged his spine, she held on. Finally, she had a clear view of what was going on.

And swore. Blacktongue stood in the same spot as before, theatrically brushing ash from his sleeve. "That might work on my soldiers, old friend, but I'm made of sterner stuff."

So Ronan struck, his huge jaws clamping on his foe. Even if Blacktongue could withstand dragon fire, he wasn't immune to dragon teeth. He let out a wail of terror as the long fangs drove home. Alana's involuntary cry was lost in the noise as the rest of the balcony gave way before crashing to the empty seats below. Ronan shook the sorcerer as a terrier would a rat. Then he flapped his wings, aiming for the Shimmer and his home.

Alana hung on, leaning into the motion. She felt a little drunk, terrified and intoxicated to be in the presence of so much raw power. At Castle Highclaw, the dragons had been polite, chatty, and almost always in their two-footed form. This was her first clue about what they could really do—and how ruthlessly they could do it.

But she shouldn't have discounted Blacktongue so fast. Ronan's nose was nearly at the Shimmer when light flared from the dragon's jaws in rays of sickly green. A moment later, there was the sudden *whump* of an explosion. Ronan spun head over tail, wings thundering in a mighty effort to right himself. Alana gripped with her heels, desperately clinging to the bony plate with both hands. Unlike the magic carpet, Ronan had no spell to keep passengers from sliding off. Alana almost made it, but as the dragon's head dipped toward the ground, she went upside down. She lost her grip and was suddenly falling, the air rushing in her ears.

She curled into a ball, crashing first into one of the tables the scorekeepers used, and then to the sandy floor. Pain exploded in her head, the world spinning and going dark by turns. She forced open her eyes, desperate to know what was happening.

Alana screamed Ronan's name as the Shimmer closed, with Blacktongue and her dragon on the other side.

❧ 18 ❧

A month later, daisies were springing up in the graveyard, littering the grass with stars of white and yellow. Summer had come, and with it long, cloudless days meant for ice cream and vacations. Being unemployed again, Alana was sort of on vacation. The prize money from the fight—the cats had lost the moment they'd fled from the fighting circle—was generous.

She touched Tina's headstone before sitting in the grass. "I got them for you. I showed the Slash what we were really made of. Hugo Martigen is dead. Tyrell is hospitalized from a very nasty fall, and he and his crew are being held for treason."

Fae law enforcement was forgiving about things like parking tickets and drinking at the beach. However, if someone crossed a major line—then it was as relentless as a banshee. Tyrell was in deep trouble, and he would only be the first under the microscope. The investigation would be broad and thorough, and it was unlikely anyone would be spared from answering questions. The fae community was in for a shake-up, but in Alana's books, that would be for the good.

"The only downside is that the Shimmer is gone," she said in a low voice. Tina had always been the one Alana had trusted with her secrets and heartbreaks. She still was. "I can't get to Ronan."

Tears pricked behind her eyes. She'd cried her heart out for weeks—had even wondered if that was literally possible—but the well of her sadness seemed never to run dry. Alana wasn't one to give in, but her fighting spirit had faded with Ronan's loss. He'd taken a piece of her with him.

She was on the brink of surrendering once more, except a shadow fell across the gravestone. Alana glanced up to see Barleycorn.

This time, he seemed rested. "Congratulations on your victory. Spectacular interruptions aside, that was well fought."

"Thanks," she said. "What are you doing here?"

"This is my first free moment since you set the world on fire. I've been meaning to speak to you privately, so here I am." He sat on the grass, heedless of his pale gray suit, and gestured around them. "I think we're free from eavesdroppers."

Alana leaned back on her hands, wishing he hadn't come so she could grieve in peace. "Do we have unfinished business?"

"Always."

"I don't understand."

"I bet on you in the fight, and if Martigen was still in business, there'd be a handsome payout." He gave a wry smile. "But then I've been betting on you for a while. I knew you could destroy that lamp, but you had to use the wish the way you did. I was counting on you living up to your reputation as the Incorruptible."

Alana's head quietly exploded. "Dude, why didn't you just tell me what to do when you came to my cell?"

"Practical reasons." He shrugged, the gesture showing off the broad shoulders beneath the exquisitely tailored jacket. "Spells like that have rules. You had to sacrifice your own interests. You can't do that if you know everything's going to turn out okay."

"That sucks!"

"Try knowing the answer that could save the day, but having to keep your mouth shut. That sucks, too."

Annoyed, Alana sat up, dusting the grass from her hands. "I'm just glad it's over. It is over, right?"

"Corruption is defeated. The arena will be repaired. There will, however, be a strict no-pets policy at the fights." He rested an arm across one knee, studying her with his blue-gold eyes. "What will you do now that the dust has settled?"

Alana sighed, and it came from the bottom of her soul. "I don't know. I'm done fighting for entertainment. When I was in the faery realm, I wanted to be part of Bright Wing's battle. It was real, and being a warrior there mattered."

"The dragons need all the help they can get."

"Maybe. Maybe not. When I first visited your office, you said I'd never meet a dragon—that they were too proud to adapt and survive. But they fought back. Against the odds, they're still there."

"You respect that." Barleycorn made it a statement, not a question.

"Of course I do. I understand it through and through."

Barleycorn fell silent for a moment, as if turning that over in his mind. "Do you wish you could have stayed with Ronan?"

"Yes." She said it without hesitation. "I'd go there now, but I can't. The mirrors don't work. I tried Corby's and Tyrell's."

"The Shimmer is Shade magic," Barleycorn said. "There are very few fae who can use it, even if they have strong magical abilities."

"Which I don't."

He sighed. "No, you don't. But I suppose we need to get you settled."

Alana wondered where he was going with this. "Are you offering me another job?"

"Absolutely not. You didn't stick with the last one I gave you. Instead, I'm going to tell you about mine."

"Now I'm really confused."

"Do you recall Morwenna?"

"My faery godmother?" Alana said without enthusiasm. "I was such a disappointment that she quit."

Barleycorn pulled a face. "Yes, she was more the bunny and bluebird sort. You were a foundling, but the elders were sure your mother was a forest fae. They thought Morwenna would be a good match."

"They were wrong."

"True. But Morwenna was correct about one thing—you were destined for something besides waiting in a tower for a princely rescue."

"No kidding."

"After that announcement, she moved on to easier clients. So, long ago, I stepped in as a substitute for Morwenna."

Alana's breath caught as shock zinged through her. "You're my faery godfather? Why didn't you say something?"

"And be victimized by a teenaged girl wanting prom dresses and pumpkin coaches?"

Alana was scandalized. "I would never!"

"Oh yes, you would have. Everyone wants to fit in at that age."

"But I..." She trailed off, sorting through a jumble of memories. "I was a disaster. And then the fights... I wasn't like I was supposed to be. It was *hard*. Why did you let me flounder like that?"

"I didn't let you flounder more than was healthy for any young person finding their way in life. I'm just too skilled to be obvious. Give me that much credit, at least." He grew serious. "Mostly, I wanted you to grow up to be your own person without magical interference."

Alana's chest was tight with a confusion of emotions—resentment, surprise, and an unexpected sense of rightness. He hadn't tried to make her something she wasn't.

"I'm glad I held back," Barleycorn said. "You became who you are now. You don't quit. You value justice and respect. Your chief strength outside the fighting circle is compassion."

"So I grew up in the school of hard knocks."

"And freed the dragon and rescued the prince, not to mention saving the world as we know it. Overall, I think I did okay as a faery godfather."

She smacked his arm. "Stop taking the credit."

"Ouch." He rubbed the spot where she'd hit. "Anyhow, I think I owe you some sparkle dust now."

Barleycorn reached into his jacket pocket, then withdrew a blue velvet jewelry box. "This is for you. It was meant as a graduation gift, but you never went to college. This seems like an even better occasion for it."

Alana opened the box. A heart-shaped pendant set with sapphires rested on a white silk pillow. "It's lovely," she said, although she couldn't think of a single place to wear something so fancy.

"It will give you command of one spell for the rest of your life, whether or not you have magical powers." He tilted his head. "No strings attached or fine print to read, but choose carefully because once your decision is made, you can't change your mind."

Alana was instantly on her feet, mind racing forward. "Can you teach me how to use mirror magic? Can I visit the dragons?"

Barleycorn's smile said he'd expected her request. "You certainly can. Your prince awaits."

"JUST DO IT," BARLEYCORN TOLD HER SEVERAL DAYS LATER, once Alana had practiced summoning the Shimmer.

She jogged from foot to foot, breathing hard from nerves. Before her stood a full-length looking glass in a stand. She could see her image, cheeks pink with excitement, the pendant flashing at her throat. She'd even dressed up for the occasion in slim black pants and a silky red blouse. "This will take me to wherever Ronan is, right?"

"Right."

"What if he's flying?"

"For the last time," Barleycorn said in quelling tones, "the spell isn't stupid. Just go."

Before she could stall a moment longer, she pressed her palm to the mirror and exhaled. Ice seemed to shoot from the pendant to her belly, radiating down her limbs. She never saw the Shimmer form when she cast the spell, but she could feel it—the sudden presence of the other side and the vast, empty gulf between.

It wasn't easy to take that first step across. Not when she had to rely on her newfound powers. Fear crawled up her chest, leaving a copper taste in her mouth. Then Alana stepped across the void.

Blackness. Cold. Solitude.

And then she was on a mountaintop, the fae realm spreading like a quilt beneath her. She raised a hand to shield her eyes. Despite the brightness of the sun, the air was cool this high up.

The mountaintop was actually a flat plateau large enough for several stone buildings. They ringed an open expanse of bare rock. She took a few steps, noticing the intricate carvings below her feet. They had a ceremonial feel, although she had no idea what the pictographs meant. Whatever this place was, it seemed very old.

A dragon roared above her. She craned her neck to see a beast with spotted wings somersaulting in the air, clearly playing in the updrafts over the valley. The beast seemed smaller than Ronan, but it was hard to tell from the ground.

"That's Fliss," said a voice. *His* voice.

Ronan stood in the arched doorway of one of the buildings, his arms spreading wide in invitation. "Hello, Alana."

"Hi!" Alana ran toward him a few steps, then hesitated. All her fears tangled inside her—she wasn't a princess, a dragon, or anybody special. Ronan wasn't her slave anymore. He didn't owe her a thing. *Why does he want me?*

She couldn't think. She could only feel, and even that was a jumble of excitement and dread and wonder and—and, oh, how she wanted Ronan so very much.

As she stopped, his arms fell and he stood with his back to the doorway. His brows drew together in a frown, as if he wasn't sure what was happening.

"Barleycorn helped me get here," she blurted. "It was about time he did something besides lurk around and play head games."

She'd planned to say something more sophisticated, though she still wasn't sure what that might have been. And then she took in Ronan's expression. It was guarded, almost devoid of emotion. How should she interpret that? Had his feelings for her changed? Or were they ever real? Now that he was free, and heir to a kingdom...

On the surface, he was the same, his sculpted features kissed by the high mountain sun. And yet, he looked weary, as if he'd kept watch too many nights in a row. Right now, he regarded her carefully, as if not certain what to do.

She wanted to tell him so much, to touch him, to hold him, but nerves pinned her where she stood. "What happened to Blacktongue?" she asked instead.

"He fought hard, but he did not survive," Ronan said, anger thick in his voice, but also a hint of satisfaction. "His forces and strongholds were demolished shortly afterward."

"Are you all right?" She came forward as well, stopping just out of reach. "That was a fierce explosion."

He shrugged, finally strolling forward. "I chipped a tooth."

"Should you see a dentist?"

He gave her a suspicious look.

"It's okay," she said, wanting nothing more than to reach out and take his handsome face between her hands. "They give you a free toothbrush. If you're good, you get a prize from their treasure chest."

Good grief, she was babbling! Still, interest kindled in his eyes. Dragons liked treasure.

But then he folded his arms, and the gesture was oddly self-protective. "There is something I need to ask. You know me as I stand here now, but in the arena, you encountered my other form for the first time."

"And what's your question?"

"After what you saw, are you afraid of dragons?" he asked. "You seem cautious now, even wary."

She laughed, and it felt like the first time she'd breathed in weeks. "You are *magnificent*."

His eyebrows went up. "But?"

"I'm not. I'm just me."

He closed the distance between them in a single step. "Once I was free, the first thing I did was come for you. I had to. Nothing matters without you."

"So you're okay that I'm here?"

Smiling softly, he reached out, cupping her cheek. "Of course, Alana. You set me free in more ways than I can name."

She opened her mouth to say more, but nothing came. The softly possessive heat in his eyes stole her words, and all her fears melted like frost in the sunshine. With a sigh, she leaned into his chest, feeling the hard strength of his body. Even in his human form, he seemed more solid now that the lamp was shattered. Finally, they were together and free.

"How is Bright Wing taking your second return?" she asked a long moment later.

"My dragon settled all doubts," he said with a smile.

She looked up into his face. "I want to hear that story."

"Let's just say matters can proceed on a solid footing. There are no secrets now, no compromises."

"They know who's boss?"

He chuckled. "Always respect the dragon."

"Perhaps you should put that on your business cards."

"Perhaps I should."

"How is your father?"

"Back on his throne and roaring orders as if he never left it. We pushed the Shades back beyond our northern borders. Once he got a taste of victory, he remembered his crown. The air fae across the land are ecstatic."

Pride and love shone in Ronan's face as he spoke, making Alana fall for him just a little more. "And you are his general again?"

"I am, though Fliss is organizing patrols over the farmlands to keep our people safe. There is no shortage of hard work to be done." Ronan swept a hand, indicating the scenery around them. "Do you know where we are?"

Alana shook her head.

"This is the Wheel."

Then she saw it—the carvings in the rock formed a circle in four quadrants that corresponded to the four fae elemental tribes: air, water, fire, and earth. "It's deserted."

"But not dead." He guided her to the center of the carvings, where a bowl was dug into the stone. "This is where the Council of the Wheel lit their beacon fire in times of trouble. It summoned the high king to bring his armies in defense of the land."

He knelt and spoke a word of power. A pale flame of magic sprang into the air. Alana blinked, mesmerized by the magical fire. This was a declaration, a bugle call that could be seen far and wide. Her warrior instincts, formerly flattened by loss, stirred back to life.

"What happens next?" she asked.

"We have a window of opportunity. Blacktongue has fallen, and the Shades must find a lackey to serve as their vizier. That was why he groomed Corby and Martigen—one of them would have eventually become the Blacktongue of your world."

"But isn't my world safe?" Alana asked. "At least for now?"

"For now. The Shades' grip is weakened, and now is the moment to strike. Rumors claim High King Jorwarth went into hiding after his defeat. It's time he returned. The air fae—Bright Wing—are ready to fight. Laren is working hard to bring the water fae to our aid. If enough faithful hearts answer, the fae will rule our realm once more."

Alana took a step back so she could meet his eyes. "I want in on that fight, if you'll have me."

Ronan didn't reply in words. He kissed her, softly at first and then with growing urgency. She'd missed the warmth of his breath against her cheek, the slide of his tongue against hers. His touch was like coming home. As if he'd read her mind, he pulled her yet closer, and the hard, hot press of his lips crumbled the last of her doubts. She was Alana, who had faced death and brought down their enemies.

Ronan had the power to remind her of who she truly was. They knew each other in all the ways that mattered. They knew their hearts.

"I love you," she finally said as she came up for air.

The beacon wasn't the only flame going. Alana's entire body suddenly burned with wanting him.

"I love you, too, my warrior." He pressed his forehead to hers. "Be my mate. I want you by my side. I want to be your partner in every way."

Happiness burst inside her, making her soul sing. "Yes. Always."

"Respect the dragon," he said softly, "but respect his mate more, for she was strong enough to break his chains."

THE END

❦

Continue the adventure with *Shatter*, the second book of the
Crown of Fae series.

❦

Get news, exclusive excerpts, and sneak peaks in my newsletter.

AFTERWORD

Thank you so much for reading *Shimmer*. It was so much fun to write, and I hope that enjoyment made it onto the page!

If you enjoyed the story, please tell a friend or leave a review. Reviews help other readers find good stories and are incredibly important to authors. Your opinion matters!

Also, if you'd like to keep up on what's happening with my books, please sign up for my newsletter on my website at www.SharonAshwood.com.

I promise that I won't share your email or information, and I won't send you spam.

If you'd like to get a peek at the next adventure in the Crown of Fae series, turn the page and meet the valiant—if slightly doomed—sea captain, Maxwell Stokes. He goes toe-to-toe with Tessa Harrison, a thoroughly modern woman hiding from a murderer, who also happens to be the fae king of the deep ocean...

SHATTER

Crown of Fae Book Two

by Sharon Ashwood

Copyright © 2019

Dawn splintered the night as Captain Maxwell Stokes recalled exactly how bad a hangover could be.

He sat on the deck of the *Solitude*, his feet propped on a crate. He wasn't sure where the chair he'd collapsed in had come from, but it didn't belong on the ship. He ached as if he'd been in an epic battle, although he couldn't recall any such thing. Worse, his mouth tasted as if he'd eaten a filthy blanket—perhaps one the ship's cat slept on right along with the rats that were her meals.

On the positive side, he'd had a glorious time at his sister Lisette's wedding—or what he could remember of it. The scatter of bottles, discarded pipes, and the sleeping crew who stretched across the deck would have to be cleared away first thing, but that would involve noise and bustle. For just a handful of seconds, he craved peace.

The *Solitude* was at anchor in Margit Bay, the tiny western city-state of Pomandine stretched along the shore. The ancient buildings crowded around the harbor, with the grander houses rising along the steep mountainside behind it. High up was the castle, the white stone made rosy by the first streaks of sunlight.

That was where Stokes had been born and where—someday, eventually—he'd return to claim his birthright.

In the meantime, Lisette and her new husband would govern in his stead. It was a love match, with good sense and compatible minds to support it. The groom was from a wealthy merchant family, ideally suited to help Lisette govern taxes and trade.

The shining happiness on his sister's face made him long for a family of his own—but his desires didn't matter. He commanded Pomandine's small war fleet, and they had joined the high king's navy in defense of the realm. Love would have to come for Stokes later—much later.

Last night's revelry was all the rest and recreation he would get.

Stokes rose, stretching his limbs to warm them against the dawn's chill. He moved across the deck, stepping carefully to avoid his sleeping men. The night sky was fading to a study in silver and pink, the scent of mountain pines on the breeze. The first of the fishing fleet was leaving the harbor, black silhouettes against the shining mirror of the sea. It was a scene that had played out every morning for a thousand years. The fleet bobbed like children's toys beside his three-decker warship, and his chest tightened with the need to protect them.

Lisette had accused Stokes of loving adventure more than his duty to his people, but she was wrong. He fought so Pomandine and its fishers and silk merchants, its fine ladies and picturesque streets, remained untouched. Like a madman, he'd pushed his crew to reach home in time for the celebration, but he could not linger. The enemy—the creatures they called Shades—pushed farther west with every battle.

Stokes had no sooner finished the thought than a movement in the water caught his eye. Between two fishing vessels, a scrap of darkness rode the waves. He squinted, wishing the dawn was brighter. Cormac Manannan, the Sea King of Faery, ruled his kingdom beneath the western waters, and the dark shape might be one of his subjects catching his morning meal. While a sighting was rare, it was nothing of concern. The ocean fae were allied with the high king's forces. And yet...

Stokes leaned against the ship's side, wishing he knew where his spyglass had got to. He strained for a better look, concern clearing his brain of the last fumes of wine. Something was not right.

That was no mermaid sporting in the waves. It was a small, lean craft cutting through the water at a magically fueled speed. It headed toward the outermost edge of the scattered fishing boats. Stokes tensed, studying the scene. There was another such boat, a bit farther south. And a third. They were circling the fishermen, deadly as any sharks.

His sour stomach, still full from the wedding banquet, nearly rebelled. He'd seen these crafts before. *Shades.* Somehow, they'd slipped through the cordon of warships and sailed here, to his home.

Stokes nudged the closest sailor with his booted foot. "Wake up!"

The man groaned, flopping to his back and shielding his eyes from the blazing sunrise.

"Find Reynolds," Stokes ordered. "Get him on his feet."

Reynolds was the first mate, well-versed in managing half-drunk sailors.

"Aye-aye, sir," the man moaned.

"There are Shades in the bay," Stokes said.

His words were like ice water. Instantly, the man clambered to his feet and gave an awkward salute. "Sir!"

Stokes reached for his sword, then remembered he'd taken it off for the dancing. His mind raced, calculating their chances. He had one ship, but where there was one Shade vessel, there were always dozens more. "Sound the summoning horns. We need the sea king's aid."

The sailor's eyes went wide as he took off at a run. Stokes

followed, shouting orders as he went to arm himself for war. He'd barely reached his cabin when the great curving war horns sounded from high up the main mast. The growl of the huge instruments reflected from the mountainsides, echoing across the water. The waves seemed to shudder with the booming grumble, sending flocks of gulls wheeling in the air. Wisely, many of the fishing vessels turned, fleeing to the safe embrace of the harbor.

Those farther out were in trouble. As soon as he returned to the deck, Stokes saw the enemy crafts had multiplied, closing around the fishing fleet. The enemy was too close to friendly vessels to use the ship's cannons, so Stokes ordered archers to employ their longbows from the round platforms positioned high up the masts. A poisoned arrow to the throat could kill a Shade when little else worked.

The archers were halfway to their positions when the first vessel went down. The *Marli Jane* was a modest size, but her white-and-green paint gleamed in the new sunlight. She was tacking hard to escape the Shade's path, white sails bellied out with the morning wind. She was fast, but not as nimble as the enemy. A ball of darkness flew through the air to land on her deck, trailing wisps of something—smoke, mist, or pure pestilence—in its wake.

A shout of horror rose from the crew of the *Solitude*. They knew what the dark ball meant. Stokes had found his spyglass, and he now trained it on the *Marli Jane*. A stain spread from where the scrap of blackness had landed, crawling outward like a creeping mold. The deck crumbled where it touched, leaving nothing but rot and powder. The crew shrank away as the planks collapsed, and the proud sails blackened to tatters. A few jumped overboard, trusting their luck to the sea. The others clung to the vanishing boat, which eventually collapsed inward as if crushed by an invisible fist.

Stokes lowered the spyglass. He'd seen the Shades' magic at work before, and it had left entire coastlines bare of life. Farther inland, they'd scoured the dragons' lands, and the farms and villages near the desert. They seemed to kill for no reason beyond the wild joy of destruction. How could he stop them here and now, on his doorstep?

The ship's archers fired, catching one of the dark-clad Shades through the shoulder. It was a good shot, especially since they were hard to see, hooded and hiding where the light was dim. The figure grabbed for the arrow, a gloved hand groping for the wound, but it collapsed to nothing, as if its cloak had been filled with air.

The *Solitude*'s crew cheered, but the victory was small. By the time they had killed a single enemy, a dozen ships had sunk. Stokes swore a vicious oath, wishing for a human enemy he could fight hand to hand—wishing for a magic spell of his own.

His curse was answered. Light bloomed from beneath the sea, spreading pools of violet, aquamarine, and sapphire through the water. The illumination came in wavering circles of brilliance, as if the ocean itself was waking.

Giant crystals broke the waves, rising on spears of gleaming gold. Then the King of the Sea himself followed, riding in a sea-green chariot. Seahorses crested the storm-tossed waves. His attendants were the merrows and merfolk, the sirens and selkies. Water streamed from them in glittering sheets, pooling in a white froth that chased the fleeing boats to the shore.

The *Solitude*'s sailors whistled and cheered. Some of the sea folk were beautiful, others wildly grotesque. Either way, Stokes had never seen such a welcome sight as Cormac Manannan rising in his chariot. The sea king was tall and heavily muscled, draped in sea-green robes. One hand held a jeweled trident, the symbol of his rule.

Stokes's heart leaped with newfound courage.

"Your Majesty," Stokes cried, waving from the deck. "We crave your aid to throw off these invaders."

"You summon me, human, according to the ancient treaties

between the high king and my people?" The sea king's voice roared with the crash of waves and the cry of gulls.

"By the fae and by the dragon, I summon you," Stokes replied, using the formal language of the old oaths. "By human's sword and goblin's hammer, I conjure you to defend the surface world. Faery is in danger, and the old alliances must rise. Help me save my people in Pomandine."

Silence fell over the merfolk. Then, a loud keening rose from the sea king's attendants, as if they mourned a death. Stokes covered his ears to block the high-pitched noise. The creatures lifted bare arms to the skies, wailing until the king silenced them with a wave of one hand.

The sound cut off abruptly. Relieved, Stokes took his hands from his ears. A bosun swore loudly, the words resonating over the water.

"Human," Cormac said, his voice grave. "The old oaths served an old world. One before this enemy plague."

Stokes gripped his brass spyglass, hands suddenly numb with dread. "What do you mean, Sea King?"

"If I give the Shades the land, they will leave the deep waters alone."

Understanding slammed into Stokes. The sea king had struck a bargain with the Shades to save his own people. The *Solitude* was doomed. So was every fishing boat on the water—along with the men, women, and children who depended on their catch.

Volcanic fury flared in Stokes's veins. "You *traitor*."

Cormac Manannan ignored him, instead pointing his trident to the north. The waves lashed higher in that direction, responding to his command.

"What's he doing?" the bosun cried.

Stokes wished he knew. The Shades had turned their boats in the same direction, abandoning the wreckage of the fishing fleet. "Fire on the bastards," he ordered.

The crew hastened to obey. Soon, the brass cannons boomed

and belched, picking off the enemy's vessels as if this were merely target practice. The Shades barely seemed interested in evasive maneuvers. The crew's cheers started out hearty, only to fade as realization set in.

The Shades were waiting as the sea king's wall of water grew higher. When it towered like a great porthole above the ocean and far, far taller than the *Solitude*'s highest mast, Manannan lowered his trident. The sun was fully up now, and the shining, churning disk of water glistened in the sun like a silver platter. Like a mirror.

Stokes almost fell to his knees in horror. He knew little of Shade magic, but he knew of the spell called the Shimmer. It worked on the principle that two reflective surfaces could form a doorway between locations or even worlds. The sea king had just made the biggest mirror ever, and Stokes would wager his best sword one of those Shade crafts held a sorcerer.

He was correct. The giant disk of water turned ink black, and a flotilla of Shade warships sailed through the Shimmer. These weren't the small, sleek runabouts that had attacked the fishermen, but massive ships with two and three decks, bristling with cannon.

"Fire on them," Stokes cried, wasting no time rallying his crew.

Even as he gave the order, his thoughts spun. With the sea king's help, the Shades had found a shortcut to the west of Faery. The innocent lives that had been safe yesterday were all but lost. Stokes gulped for breath, suddenly finding it hard to get air. Had he somehow invited this disaster by leaving his post for the wedding? Had he failed in his duty? The idea was emotionally true, but logically ridiculous. He hadn't caused this, but the fact he'd taken a moment for pleasure savaged him with razor claws.

There was no more time for guilt. The *Solitude*'s guns fired, punching holes high in the deck of the nearest Shade vessel. It was all but futile—the odds were wildly against them—but defiance was all they had left.

Until they lost even more. The King of the Sea struck the waves with his trident, and the earth began to shake. Stokes spun to face the shore—to face Pomandine, where his sister and her new husband slept in their castle bedroom high on the mountainside. The city was his childhood, his anchor, his once and future home.

The three Shade warships had fanned out, training their cannons on the city. For a panicked moment, Stokes wondered if the *Solitude* was in the line of fire, but then realized they would miss the ship on either side. Then, as the three ships fired their cannons, Stokes wished he'd already been blown to smithereens.

There were no lead balls, no volleys of shot, but the guns fired *something* he couldn't see. It hit with a clap that sent the crew staggering as the ship pitched in response. Then, with an indescribable thunder of falling stone, the whole of the mountainside that held Stokes's world slid into the sea, taking the piers and harbor with it. Boats crumpled beneath the avalanche. Pillars of dust rose to the clouds. Even through the crash of destruction, Stokes could hear his people screaming.

Within seconds, there was nothing but bare mountainside and rubble. It looked as if a god had wiped the rock face clean. The crew of the *Solitude* fell deathly silent. Even the sea king and his people remained still as statues—at least for the moment it took to understand what had happened.

Then the wave came. A city had fallen into the ocean. All the displaced water had to go somewhere. The sea king plunged beneath the waves, fleeing to safety with his people. The Shade ships vanished into a tower of water, but the *Solitude* seemed to catch the crest, rising higher and higher as the ship was hurtled back toward the Shimmer.

Perhaps it was the sea king's magic that kept them from capsizing. Stokes didn't know, but he would seize this chance to retaliate. He grabbed the tiller, steering straight into the portal the Shades had used.

"Captain." The helmsman clutched his arm. "What are you thinking?"

The man had no right to question his superior, but Stokes answered anyway. "Tell the gunners to fire every barrel of powder in the hold once we hit the Shimmer. Sacrifice is the only duty we have left."

It was a fancy way of saying they were about to die.

❦

The story continues in *Shatter*, Book Two of the Crown of Fae series.

ABOUT THE AUTHOR

USA Today Bestselling author Sharon Ashwood is a novelist, desk jockey and enthusiast for the weird and spooky. She has an English literature degree but plays with numbers for her living. Interests include insulating the walls with her to-be-read books and building a graveyard diorama over much of her desk. As a vegetarian, she freely admits the whole vampire/werewolf fantasy would never work out, so she writes paranormal romances instead.

Sharon is a winner of the RITA® Award for Paranormal Romance. She lives in the Pacific Northwest and is owned by a pair of naughty black cats.

www.SharonAshwood.com
Sharon@SharonAshwood.com

Dragon Lords novellas

Lord Dragon's Conquest

Valkyrie's Conquest

Audiobook

Enchanted Warrior

Corsair's Cove miniseries

Kiss in the Dark

Secret Seed

Long Road Home